The BEGINNING of FOREVER

THE SUMMER UNPLUGGED SERIES

CHAPTER 1

There are few things more terrifying than thinking you might be pregnant at the age of eighteen. One of the things that makes that more terrifying list? The two minutes after you pee on a stick and watch it turn pink. My stomach crawled into my throat and I had to blink my eyes several times so I could see. Only my hands were so shaky I couldn't focus on the stupid pee stick. It was pink. Faintly and then all at once it was very dark. Pink in three places.

Of course I knew what three pink lines meant. I had read the package a dozen times before I even opened it and yet, I still had to check it again. I set the stick on the counter, briefly reminding myself to clean off the pee drips later, and grabbed the box to read the instructions again.

Yep. It still said the same thing. Three lines - pregnant.

Maybe this one is defective.

"Babe? The suspense is killing me." There was a tap on the other side of the bathroom door and then a thud of what sounded like Jace's forehead resting against it.

"Just a second," I called back. My voice didn't even sound like me. It felt like me, the real me, was somewhere far away watching the other me, the Bayleigh who is sitting on the toilet, yoga pants around her ankles, and thinking, "Wow, I'm glad I'm not her."

Only I am her. And this is my life now.

Oh my God. Oh. My. God.

Mom is gonna kill me.

Mom. I'm going to be a mom.

I try to swallow and I almost choke on my own spit. My vision blurs and I rush to stand and tug up my pants and smooth out my shirt and try to look normal. I wash my hands and toss the box into the trash can. The mirror above the sink shows a girl who is too pale, too scared, too...unprepared.

"You alive in there?" He's trying to sound all light-hearted. I know he's freaking out just as badly as I am, but he won't show it. He never loses his cool around me.

"Yeah," I call back, staring at the door and trying to picture what he looks like on the other side of it. "I'm alive."

"Everything okay?" Those two words were a secret code. An encrypted message that actually meant so much more than just *is everything okay*. It meant, *am I about to be a father?*

My reply was just as cryptic.

"Yeah."

CHAPTER 2

If there's one thing I hate more than morning sickness, it's shopping.

Okay, maybe hate is a little too harsh for something that isn't that big of a deal. Even though I'm a girl and girls are supposed to love shopping and all that, I've never been that much of a fan. Probably because Mom and I never had any money when I was growing up, so shopping was always a lackluster event that left me pining for beautiful things that we would never be able to take home.

I am eighteen years old now and recently moved out of my mom's house and into an apartment with my boyfriend–er, I mean fiancé–Jace. (It's still really weird calling him that. We've only been engaged for a month and I've only had my engagement ring for two weeks because he had it custom designed and that took forever.) Anyway, back to shopping. Things have changed a ton in the last few months of my life. Now, I no longer have to worry about money when I go shopping. Nope. I have a shiny clear plastic debit card with my name on it.

Only I still can't seem to use it without getting this

instant knot in my stomach because, despite what Jace constantly tells me, the money in our joint bank account is not mine. It's all Jace's money. Every last digital penny. He earned it at his job or by winning some motocross race, or by attending fancy motocross events that pay him around five grand a night just to show up and mingle. And the fact that he claims it's my money too just because I'm going to marry him in a few months, doesn't really make the money feel like mine. I didn't do anything to earn it.

Of course last time I said something like that was a few weeks ago when we were hanging out in our apartment watching television. I was sprawled out across the couch with my head in his lap because usually when I do that, he'll absentmindedly play with my hair while he watches sports and I am a total sucker for having my hair petted like I'm some kind of housecat.

A commercial came on and it was advertising these stupid As Seen on TV blankets that lit up and had furry animal faces on them. It was one of the most useless household items ever, but the pink bunny one just spoke to me.

"Oh my God, I neeeeeed one," I had said in a sing-song voice. Jace stopped stroking my hair as he leaned forward and took his wallet out of his back pocket. "Do you have your phone?" he asked, pointing toward the TV. "It says you can order online."

"Psh, I'm not going to order one," I said. "I don't really need it, it's just cute."

"You need it," he said, digging through his wallet and retrieving a debit card. This was a few days before he had requested a second debit card with my name on it. "You'd look adorable all wrapped up in that thing."

I shook my head against his lap. "I don't want you paying for it."

"Not this again," he said, poking me in the forehead. I swatted his hand away, but he poked me again just to be annoying.

"I'm grateful that you want to buy me stuff, but I didn't earn any of that money. I don't feel right spending it."

"Get over it, Bay." His phone was suddenly in his hand and he squinted at the TV and then typed in a URL into the web browser. "I'm buying this damn blanket and you're going to love it."

I groaned. "I don't want you to waste money on crap just because I want it," I said. "You already pay all of our bills. It's just not fair."

He frowns. "I wish you wouldn't see things that way. You are going to be my wife. What's mine is yours."

I couldn't help but smile. "And what's mine is yours," I said, grabbing his hand.

"Well that's good, because this morning I used your shampoo because mine was all out."

"I thought you smelled a little girly today." He rolled his eyes and I stuck out my tongue and the moment was over, changed and forgotten.

Money is hardly the issue about my shopping woes today. Nope. Money doesn't have anything to do with it. I swallow back a mountain of anxiety as I climb out of my car and step forward. The building in front of me is one that I've seen a million times just passing by, and honestly, I never thought I'd ever visit a place like this. And, even if in my wildest dreams I had imagined I'd be in a place like this, it would have been with my best friend. As my terrible luck would have it, Becca got called into work for some emergency BMX thing and had to cancel on me at the last minute. I know she loves her job and I know her boss relies on her to keep things running smoothly at C&C BMX track, so I just suck it up and try to deal. I won't let my disappointment sour my day. Becca feels bad enough already, and it really wasn't her fault. Besides, I tell myself- I am a big girl. I can do this.

Butterflies flip around in my stomach and I briefly wonder how there's even room in there for butterflies since, well, a baby is also growing in my body. But when it comes to emotional turmoil, I guess there's always room. I take a deep breath and tell myself to calm down.

Sure, I am about to purchase something I'll only use once in my life and it will cost more money than I've ever spent at one time, but when you break it down to its barest form—it's just shopping.

Wedding dress shopping.

I take a deep breath and grab the silver ornate handle of Elizabeth's Bridal and enter.

A tall woman with wavy red hair greets me when I walk into the boutique. She wears a slender pencil skirt and black pumps that would surely break my neck if I wore them, but she glides effortlessly across the carpeted floor, extending a hand toward me.

"Welcome to Elizabeth's Bridal. I am Mackenzie. You must be my three o'clock," she croons. "Bayleigh?"

"Yes ma'am," I say. She isn't that much older than I am, but this seems like the kind of store in which you call women ma'am. The carpet is white, the walls are white with pearly patterned wallpaper, the furniture is white and all of it just screams luxury and class and fancy-rich-people. I am a little, *okay a lot*, over my head here. The entirety of my experience in dress shopping lies at the prom stores in the mall. But I stand up straight and press my shoulders back and act like I am not a terrified teenager who really really wishes I hadn't come here alone.

Mackenzie pulls up my information on her computer and readies a pearly white folder with my name on it. She says we'll put all of my measurements and information in there, but I'm barely listening. All I can do is think about how all of this would be much easier with my best friend by my side. Maybe I should reschedule for another day.

The door opens again and I turn around expecting to see another bride-to-be coming to pick out her perfect wedding dress, but it is so much better than that.

"Bay!" My smiling best friend waves and rushes over to me, wearing a lime green BMX shirt. My heart erupts into joy at seeing her here. She throws her arms around me and I'm such a dork I think I jump up and down a little.

"How did you get out of work?" I ask. Becca smirks, putting her hands on her hips. "I told my boss to shove it."

"No you didn't."

She shrugs. "Okay, maybe I didn't. But I did beg and beg and beg until he got sick of me and said I could leave."

"You're the best."

She brushes her brown hair over her shoulder and rolls her eyes up to the ceiling. "Girl, I know it."

MACKENZIE IS UNFAILINGLY PATIENT WITH US AS SHE PULLS dress after dress off the racks and presents them to me for consideration. After half an hour, we have chosen seven dresses to be added to the try-on pile and rejected another two dozen. Or maybe it was three dozen. For all I know, time has frozen in this bridal shop and the world is nothing but white silk and lace and ruffles and veils.

Mackenzie has me slip into a fitting room that's as big as my bedroom back at Mom's house and then she and two of her assistants take turns violating my privacy as they slip me into the first dress, poking and pushing all my parts until the sleeveless bodice gets laced up the back and sucks in my stomach, making my boobs look huge.

I yell at Becca to close her eyes as we emerge from the fitting room, both because I want it to be a surprise for her, but I'm also just mega nervous to be seen in a wedding dress by someone who actually knows me. She does as she's told, covering her eyes with her hands and Mackenzie leads me to a circular podium in the middle of an array of mirrors. I step up onto it and immediately feel like a princess as I stare at the five reflections of me in the angled mirrors.

"You can open your eyes," I tell Becca. "But no laughing!"

"Why would I laugh?" she says, but even with my warning glare, she bursts into giggles when she sees me for the first time. I put my hands on my hips and purse my lips. "Sorry," she says, "I don't mean to laugh, I just–" She stands and gnaws on her bottom lip. "You just look really awesome. And this is crazy. You're getting *married*, Bay."

"It's not crazy it's…"

"It's love," Makenzie supplies the missing word for me. I'm sure she's just saying that because it's her job to make the clients happy and besides, she has a big commission riding on me buying of her dresses today. So of course she's going to say things to make sure I don't ditch on getting married, but her words still bring me comfort. Jace and I don't have a typical teenager relationship and we never have. Maybe that's what makes us special.

I drop my hands from my hips and splay them out in front of the satin dress. "What do we think of this one?"

"It's nice," Becca says, walking around me to get the full effect. "But it's a little…."

"It's too blah," I say, nodding. "Plus I don't think I want a strapless dress. I'm already freaking out that my boobs will fly out of this thing and we're not even in public."

We try on a few more dresses, and when I say we, I mean *we*. Just because I'm wearing the dress doesn't mean it's a solitary affair. The boutique women have to help me into and out of every single dress. It's like these things were created to be worn with an entourage.

A little while later, I'm standing in front of the mirrors again, wearing a dress with lace sleeves that go down to my wrists and feeling like an old lady. "I'm sorry I'm being so difficult, but I'm just not sure I like any of these," I tell Mackenzie. She swats away my words with her hand. "No worries, hun. You are not being difficult at all. You should see some of the women who come in here." She glances at her assistants and they both animatedly agree. "Would you like to look around some more and find a dress that speaks to you?"

I nod but it looks more like a shrug. Honestly, I'm kind of over trying on wedding dresses. At what point is this supposed to be fun?

Becca must sense my frustration because she says, "Picture your perfect dress and describe it to me and I'll go find it."

I close my eyes for a second and try to think. "Well, I don't want it to be sleeveless but I also don't want sleeves. And this satin fabric reminds me of prom dresses and I want my dress to be an elegant gown, you know? Not just silky smooth like a prom dress." My eyes open and I look into the mirror again. "And, I don't know...maybe some kind of sparkle?"

"Got it!" Becca's voice came from across the room. I hadn't even noticed that she had left her spot by the mirrors until she comes rushing up carrying a dress over her arms. Her cheeks are flushed in excitement as she holds out the dress toward me. "It's your size. Try it on!"

Her enthusiasm is contagious and I trust her with my

life, so of course I'll trust her with a dress. I don't even look at it longer than a split second before I hand it to Mackenzie and rush back into the massive fitting room and start stripping out of the long sleeved old lady dress.

This dress is so much quicker to get into. It's simple and sleek. It has a silk lining and a lace overlay that drapes to the floor. It doesn't exactly have sleeves, so much as delicate lace triangles that cover my shoulders and keep the dress supported so I don't have to worry about having wardrobe malfunctions as I walk down the aisle.

And then there's the best part. The sparkle.

Tiny shimmery beads embellish the dress from head to toe. It sparkles and swooshes around my ankles and fits like a dream. I am in love with the most handsome man ever and this is the most beautiful dress in the world. Both of these were meant to be mine.

"I'm thinking you won't be trying on any more dresses today," Mackenzie says with a coy smile.

I smile and push open the fabric curtain of the dressing room, eager to show Becca. "I'm thinking the same thing."

CHAPTER 3

All of that dress shopping must have worn me out because at some point I wake up on the couch. Checking the time on my phone, I realize it's only six in the afternoon and I must have dozed off while watching TV. Jace hadn't been home when I got back because he was teaching a private motocross lesson with a client. But that was probably for the best because I would have been a hyperactive maniac, filled with excitement over my dress. Sometimes, when I get that way, all super excited and gushing about something girly, I'll immediately feel embarrassed as hell when I realize how childish I'd been acting. And now more than ever, I need to act mature.

I stretch and yawn from my spot on the couch and that's when the smell hits me. Jace is in the kitchen and he's cooking my favorite dinner, which is actually breakfast food. Maple flavored bacon sizzles in the frying pan and the faint scent of scrambled eggs topped with cheese fills the air. On any other day, the incredibly generous act of cooking my favorite food mixed with the delicious aroma would have made me one happy girl.

Today, though, it makes me throw up.

Jace calls after me, asking if I'm okay as I barrel down the hallway and into the bathroom, just barely making it in time to avoid spewing Diet Coke and lunch all over the place. The vomiting doesn't last very long, but my eyes fill with tears. Jace taps on the door. "You okay? Can I come in?"

"No!" I call out, slamming my hand to the back of the bathroom door to prevent him from slipping in uninvited. I twist the lock on the door for good measure and then turn on the water in the sink to brush my teeth. "I'm okay," I say.

"I'm getting tired of talking to you through bathroom doors," Jace mutters.

"Then stop doing it and go back to the kitchen." I don't mean for my voice to sound so bitchy, but I'd really really like it if he would just leave. I only like Jace seeing me when I'm cute. Brushing out the vomit stank from my mouth is decidedly *not* cute.

The nausea leaves just as quickly as it had come, and when I emerge with winter fresh breath, I feel fine again. The bacon smells good and I'm hungry. Thank God. I would have hated to turn down his dinner and hurt his feelings.

Jace seems a little annoyed when I set my plate of food on the counter and take up the barstool next to him. "What's wrong, honeybun?" I nudge him with my shoulder, smiling all stupid and dorky so he'll brighten up.

He just shakes his head and shovels a bite of food into his mouth. "Nothing."

"Sure doesn't seem like nothing." I nudge him again. "Why won't you talk to me?"

"Why won't *you* talk to *me*?" he retorts. His jaw clenches like it does when he's pissed off at bad drivers or can't fix a problem on his dirt bike. A mild panic flashes through me and I skim through everything that's happened in the last few days, trying to think of a time when I hadn't talked to him. Surely I'm not accidentally keeping any kind of secret from him? I shake my head, more to myself, and say, "I don't know what you're talking about, but I don't like you being all mad at me right now."

His face softens. "I'm talking about what just happened. You were passed out asleep for several hours, which is really weird of you to do, and then you jump up and run to the bathroom and won't talk to me about it." He grabs my hand and rubs his thumb across my palm. "I just wish you'd talk to me. What happened back there? I worry about you."

That tiny wave of panic disappears with the realization that nothing is actually wrong with Jace. He's just being paranoid. "There's nothing to talk about, babe. I was just tired from shopping all day with Becca." It's a little bit of the truth and also a little bit of a lie. I was tired because I kept waking up all night long, frazzled from these weird stress dreams of dying babies and broken engagements. But I force a smile and act like everything is okay. I can't tell Jace about the bad dreams. He'll just worry even more and he doesn't need to be worried. I'm the weirdo with the crazy imagination that likes to think up nightmarish situations with which to plague my dreams.

That nap was the best thing to happen to me today. I didn't dream at all. At least, if I did, I don't remember it.

I slide off my barstool and step closer to Jace. His knees drift apart to let me step between his legs as I slide my hands up his chest and around his shoulders. When he sits on the barstool like this, he's almost as short as I am. I press my forehead to his. "Please don't worry so much about me," I whisper, glad to have wintery fresh breath while I'm this close to him. "I think I just had like...morning sickness? But it's in the evening? I don't know, but it wasn't a big deal and I feel fine now, I promise."

Jace's eyebrows narrow. "Why can't you just tell me that in the first place?"

I shrug. "Because it's embarrassing?"

"It is not embarrassing."

I roll my eyes and pull away, pressing my finger to his nose. "Yes it is."

"Just tell me next time, okay? Don't make me freak out."

"Fiiiiine," I sigh, sitting back on my barstool. "I promise to tell you next time my body does something embarrassing, even though it's freaking embarrassing and I don't want you to know."

Jace nods approvingly. "That's all I ask."

LATER, I LIE SNUGGLED UP UNDER THE COMFORTER OF THE bed I get to share with Jace every night. It's been a month since I moved in with him after graduation, and it still surprises me nearly every day. I'll think I'm finally settled into my new apartment with him and that I'm finally getting into a daily routine of life and then suddenly it'll hit me like a light bulb clicking on over my head: *I am engaged to Jace Adams and I finally get to live with him.* No matter how many times it happens, I still get a rush of emotions that fill me up until I think I'll explode. My life is awesome in that way.

Even though I'm still scared to death of having a baby —life is still good. At least I have Jace by my side.

It's nearly midnight but I'm not sleepy, thanks to that unexpected nap from earlier. My stomach flip-flops when

Jace emerges from the shower with a black towel wrapped around his hips. The fluttering sensation in my stomach is not from morning sickness this time. It's the literal pitter-patter of a heart watching the hottest guy alive walk up to her bed. He runs a hand through his damp hair, slinging tiny droplets of water all over me. Even as I gag and squeal and throw my pillow at him for getting me all wet, I still get goosebumps when he drops the towel, slides into boxers and jumps on top of me on the bed.

"Can't...breathe..." I gasp, slapping him on the back so he'll get off me. He laughs and rolls off, allowing me to breathe again.

"You're a butt face," I say, calling him by my affection-ately insulting nickname.

"Takes one to know one," he says, leaning forward to kiss me on the forehead before turning on the small televi-sion in the corner of our room. I snuggle up against his shoulder. "So tell me about your dress," Jace says. His voice makes his chest hum under my ear.

"You know I can't tell you! It's bad luck for the groom to see the dress."

"Aw, you can't even describe it?"

I shake my head. "Nope. I refuse to bring any bad luck into this marriage."

He chuckles and brushes my hair out of my eyes. "I guess I'll survive."

Now that we're on the subject, I realize that choosing my wedding dress is just one completed task out of a list of a bazillion things to do. "Are you sure we can pull off this wedding by August ninth?"

"Of course. That's two months away." He flips chan-nels, searching for something worth watching so late at night. "Two months is a long time."

"Yeah but most people take a year or more to plan a wedding."

He scoffs. "That's way too long. People who take that long just don't love each other enough so they try to prolong it as long as they can."

"Says the wedding expert?" I say, poking him in the chest.

"Do you want to push back the date?" I can tell by the tone of his voice that he wants my answer to be no. And that's one of the most romantic things ever. I shake my head. "No way. I want to marry you now. While I'm still thin enough to fit in that dress. It's just...scary."

He stiffens. "Getting married?"

"No, God no." I smile and squeeze my arms around him, nuzzling into his chest. "It's scary trying to plan all of this stuff and also deal with the fact that we're having a baby. I mean...that's kind of a huge deal and I feel like my brain can't even focus on it yet until the wedding is over."

"I'm here when you need me," Jace says, still stroking my hair. "We're going to get through this. Things are crazy but they're a good crazy."

His words make me feel instantly better. "Well we have my dress and we've picked a date. Now we need your tuxedo. Do you want me to make you an appointment or should we wait until your best man can go with you? When is he coming, by the way?" Jace's best man will be his best friend, who I've never even met. They grew up together in California and still remain close, although they haven't seen each other since Jace moved to Texas. It works out well because I only wanted Becca to be in my bridal party and Jace only wanted one friend as well, so we'll have a symmetrical wedding party of exactly two people who are important to us.

"Do we really need an appointment for something like that? Can't we just stop by and pick one up?"

I lift up on my elbow and give him a look that suggests he was dropped on his head as a kid. "Of course you have to make an appointment. You have to try them on and pick one out."

Now he gives me the same look. "Why? A tux is a tux."

I groan. "You want to pick out the perfect tux, babe. It's not as easy as grabbing a pair of sweatpants at the sporting goods store."

"I guess you're right, but here's the deal: No one will be looking at me on our wedding day. They'll be looking at you."

"Yeah well *I'll* be looking at you, so you better look nice."

Jace's smile melts into a goofy grin. I nuzzle against him. He slides his hand over my stomach, pausing for a fraction of a second. I know we're both thinking about the baby. I don't know what to say or do. Thinking about the very real fact that a child is growing inside me is crazy and scary and also wonderful. But mostly scary. I swallow and change the subject. "You should call your best man and see if he can come visit soon. I'll make an appointment for your tuxedo fitting. And I'd really like to get him to meet Becca so we can all know each other before the day of the wedding."

"That's a good idea," Jace says, grabbing his phone from the nightstand. He pulls up a new text and sends it to some guy named Nolan.

My eyebrows draw together in confusion. "I thought your best man was named Park?" I ask, trying not to be startled. I don't know much about Jace's life from before he met me, and the idea that I've been imagining his best friend from childhood as a completely different person is unsettling. Jace shakes his head as he types out a text. "His first name is Nolan. We call him Park. We all call each other by our last names."

"Ah, okay," I say, relieved. As I watch him text, I see the tiny little square image of Park, er, Nolan, saved in Jace's phone.

"He's kind of cute," I say, squinting to see the image better. "Is he single?"

"Hey now," Jace says, pressing the phone against his chest. "You can't be leaving me for my best friend. Besides, that guy isn't nearly as fast as I am on a dirt bike." He sticks out his tongue and goes back to typing out his text message. The boy's texting ability is incredibly slow compared to mine.

"*No*," I say, rolling my eyes. "I meant for Becca. He looks like the type of guy she's always crushing on at the BMX park."

"He's single," Jace confirms. "But he lives the Cali lifestyle. I'm not sure any girl can make him settle down."

"I'm not saying I want them to fall madly in love and get married by Christmas. I'm just thinking that it could be fun to go on double dates and stuff. Plus, I can guarantee you that the moment Becca lays eyes on him, she'll be pulling me aside and begging to know if he has a girlfriend."

Jace's phone lights up with a new text and he reads over it. "Looks like you'll have a chance to play matchmaker soon. He's coming down in two weeks."

CHAPTER 4

Rain pours down on my car's windshield as I sit huddled up in the driver's seat, the heater blowing furiously on my feet and face. It's in the middle of summer, yet the thunderstorm has brought cooler weather with it and I am freezing. I turn off the windshield wipers since I don't really need to see in front of me because I'm parked at the back of the parking lot at my ob-gyn. Mondays at ten in the morning must be some kind of popular day to visit the doctor, because the parking lot is full. I can't even see another open spot so I don't know what Jace will do when he gets here.

This isn't exactly the way I had hoped to start out such an exciting day. I am officially twenty weeks pregnant and my doctor has scheduled my first ultrasound. He said if we're lucky, we'll be able to tell the baby's gender. I know some people decide to keep it a secret until the day their child is born, but that idea never even crossed my mind. I am dying to know if we're having a girl or a boy.

Mrs. Fisher, my friend at Mixon Motocross Park where Jace works, told me that women usually have an intuition that tells them if they're having a boy or a girl. She said that when she was pregnant with Teig, she knew he was a boy before she had even taken a pregnancy test. I don't know, though. I think she's crazy. I can sit here all day with my eyes closed and concentrate on my stomach, hand pressing just below my belly button, and no matter how hard I try, I can't channel any sort of intuition. This thing could be a boy or a girl or triplets or even an alien and I would have no idea.

I really, really hope it's not an alien.

The time on my car's radio says I have just seven minutes until my appointment but I can't go inside yet. Not without Jace. Not while it's raining. I skim the parking lot looking for his truck, but he still hasn't arrived. He had two big name clients schedule training sessions with him this morning but they had started at six a.m. and Jace had promised me that he'd be done in time to catch my appointment. He swore he wouldn't be late and he wouldn't miss it. As I watch the minutes pass by on the digital clock screen, I'm starting to worry.

The rain continues to pour from the sky without any sign of letting up. I sigh. Running through the parking lot in the rain is about the last thing I want to do right now, next to walking inside the doctor's office without Jace by my side. I try calling him for the third time since I've been in this parking lot. Again, he doesn't answer.

I take a deep breath, discouraged. I don't want to be mad at him, but I'm running out of ways to comfort myself and try to convince my heart that this isn't a big deal. He gets paid a lot of money for teaching motocross lessons and that money goes to support us, after all. It's his money that will pay for my doctor visit today. So I shouldn't be mad. I'm not allowed to be mad.

I shove my phone and car keys in my purse, then zip it

closed and hug it to my chest as I prepare to make a run across the parking lot in the rain. I make a mental note to get an umbrella, like any normal adult would have in their car, draw in a deep breath, and run.

Rain soaks my jeans instantly, latching onto the bottom hem and then rising up my legs until I can feel cold wet denim up to my calves. My hair is soaked, and cold, and my makeup is probably completely washed off by the time I reach the double glass doors that lead to the ob-gyn's office.

People stare at me as I burst through the doors, but I try to ignore them. The waiting room is cold and smells like some kind of awful air freshener in a can and the scent makes my stomach clench up, nauseated. I make my way through the various armchairs and couches that line the eclectically decorated waiting room and stand in line behind two women at the front counter. I glance around the room and see the curious or bored faces of all the women around me. They are old. Well, older. No one looks even close to my age. Three of the women have big pregnant bellies as they sit next to their husbands on the couches. One of the women meets my eye and I quickly turn away. I wish Jace was here.

Finally, it's my turn at the front desk.

"Hi," I say to the woman behind the counter. She's wearing pink Support Breast Cancer scrubs and flipping through paperwork. "Um, I have an appointment at ten with Doctor Qi."

"Sign in." At first I'm not even sure she's talking to me but then she reaches up and shoves a clipboard toward me. I take the attached pen and sign my name. I don't know what to do next so I just stand there a moment. When she looks up again, she seems surprised to see me still standing there. "You can have a seat."

"Thanks," I mumble as heat rushes to my face. I should have known to sit down. I mean, that's what everyone else in this waiting room is doing. I'm such an idiot without Jace. He would have known what to do. I check my phone again, but still nothing. No messages, no Jace, and nowhere to sit.

Taking a spot near the corner, I lean my back against the wall and stare out the window toward the parking lot. It's still raining and I don't see Jace's truck anywhere. He should be here. I try to calm myself and think happy thoughts, but every time something like this happens, my mind always rushes to the worst possible conclusion.

Jace is dead, crushed underneath his truck in some massive collision. Or he's fallen in love with some random woman at a gas station and now he's writing me a note to leave taped to the front door of our former apartment, telling me he's leaving me forever and to have a nice life.

Someone's voice catches my attention, pulling me out of my stupid daydreams. "Walter, go tell them they need more chairs out here so this girl can sit down." A woman with a mass of thick brown and grey curls shoves the man sitting next to her. She smiles at me and nods toward me with her thumb. "They have this poor girl standing up, and she'll probably be here for a while. It ain't right."

Walter shakes his head after giving me an appraising once-over behind his thick-rimmed glasses. "She's a kid. She's fine. Standing ain't going to hurt her one bit."

The woman leans over and touches my arm. "Honey, I'd give you my seat but I got bad knees."

"Oh thank you, but I'm fine," I say in my friendly voice, all thoughts of Jace having been shoved to the back of my mind."

"See?" Walter huffs. "Just a kid."

They're the only people talking in the waiting room,

which was quiet before Walter spoke up, and suddenly all eyes are on me and our conversation. I stare at the floor and gnaw on my bottom lip, wishing for the billionth time that my fiancé would get here already.

A hushed whisper comes from my right and although I don't turn my head, or even acknowledge that I had heard, it was obviously directed at me. Chills prickle up my arms and my heart jumps around my chest. Warm tears threaten to fill my eyes but I blink them back. A thousand rude, snappy insults come to me but I don't say any of them. I don't want to cause a scene. The last thing I need is to be kicked out of my own doctor's office for bitch-slapping a woman in the waiting room.

So I stand against the wall for the next thirty-three minutes and keep my mouth shut. When the nurse opens the side door and calls out a name, the woman who had whispered stands up and follows her to the back. Once she's gone, I let out a breath I'd been holding. My phone vibrates and I jump to read the new message, hoping to God it's from Jace.

But it isn't. It's Becca.

Becca: How's it going? Do we know if I have a boy or a girl to look forward to yet?

Me: Still waiting. Jace isn't here and I had the worst thing happen just now. I'm trying not to cry.

Becca: OMG what happened?

I don't know why it's so embarrassing admitting what happened to Becca. She's my best friend, and she's also completely aware of the situation I am in. It's not like the pregnancy is some secret or anything, so why does it make my fingers shake when I text her the story?

Me: Some lady was in the waiting room & she said "oh look, another knocked-up teenager to drain my tax dollars on her bastard baby"

Becca: What the actual hell.

Becca: I'm going to kill that witch.

Becca: What did you say? Did you slap the hell out of her?

Me: I just stood here. Like an idiot. :(

Becca: I'm sorry, Bay. I love you. Screw her. She doesn't know anything. You and your hot ass future husband won't go anywhere near her tax dollars. I bet she works as a stripper anyway.

The woman's comment still stings, but Becca's texts puts a smile on my face. I love how she's always immediately on my side, ready to insult any random stranger just to make me feel better. Now if only Jace would walk through the doors....I glance over hoping to see my wish come true, but the doors are unmoving.

It's nearly another hour later when I am finally called back into the exam room. A nurse with short black hair and tiny pink flower tattoos on her wrist leads me into the room. She's friendly and smiles at me when she talks so I've already decided that I like her. She's the first non-judgmental person I've met at this place, besides my doctor.

"I apologize for the wait," she says, tearing off the tissue paper roll from the examination bed and pulling out another sheet of it for me. "Dr. Qi had to do an emergency delivery and that's put him behind a couple of hours."

"It's okay," I mumble. It's almost as if fate knew Jace would be late and purposely made my doctor late as well. Only Jace isn't here yet. *Thanks for nothing, fate.*

She smiles again and hands me a paper gown. "Everything off," she says. "Dr. Qi will be here in a minute."

"Everything?" I stammer, feeling my face flush again.

She nods. "Get used to it, dear. All privacy goes out the

window when you have a baby." She winks at me and then she's gone, closing the door behind her.

Quickly, I slip out of my clothing and kick them into a moderately neat pile on top of a chair in the corner of the room. I try not to think about how in an ideal world with perfect situations, Jace would be sitting in that chair right now, holding my clothes for me and saying comforting things. Things like, "You totally don't look like a fat cow, I promise!"

I jump when the door opens and my doctor comes inside. He noticeably glances around the room looking for someone else. His brows furrow as he sits on the rolling chair at the foot of the bed on which I am sitting, covered in my paper gown. "Are you alone today?"

I nod. My throat is too dry to say anything.

He peers at my file. "Today is your ultrasound appointment, yes? Most women bring someone to watch the first ultrasound." He offers me a pity smile as he glances through my chart. "Ah, yes," he says, as if he's been reminded of something. "Jace is your boyfriend, correct? Are things still...okay with you two?"

I nod again and hold out my left hand, letting the gorgeous custom designed engagement ring speak for itself. This makes Dr. Qi burst into a big grin. "I am so happy for you!" he says, and it feels like a huge weight has been lifted from the room. I know he wasn't trying to feel sorry for me, but he did anyhow.

I somehow manage to find my voice. "Jace had to work today and he was supposed to be here but I'm thinking he got held up."

"That's too bad," he says.

After what is a super uncomfortable and totally awkward examination by my doctor, they move me into another room with the ultrasound technician. She's a woman barely older than I am and she smells like vanilla perfume and Skittles. She introduces herself as Jessica and she doesn't even mention how I'm alone or how I'm a teenager. For some reason, the simple act of not judging me makes me want to talk to her and explain myself. Yet when people do judge me, all I can do is sit there quietly and wish they'd go away.

"My fiancé couldn't make it today because of work," I say, watching her squirt a bottle of warm clear goo on my stomach. "I'm really annoyed that I have to be here alone."

"Totally," she says. "At least he's just working. Some guys are way too squeamish and refuse to look at the ultrasounds."

"Seriously? It's just a grainy photo on a computer screen...it's not like you're going to cut me open and poke at my organs."

This makes her laugh. She presses the ultrasound wand thing to my stomach and moves it around. Almost instantly I can hear a fuzzy thumping sound, rapid like a humming-bird's wings. "There's your heartbeat," she says. I close my eyes and listen to the sound of another human's heart beating inside my body. It is a beautiful, crazy, amazing sound.

And then it's interrupted by the heavy knocking on the door. "What the hell?" Jessica hisses. "I'm so sorry," she says to me as she storms to the door of the room and opens it just an inch. She immediately berates the person at the door and I'm grateful for it. Whoever chose to knock during my special moment should be chastised. Then to my horror, she swings the door wide open.

And Jace rushes inside.

"Jace!" In my excitement, I almost jump off the table but then I remember that my pants are pulled down a few inches and my stomach is covered in goo and disposable paper towels. So I throw my arms up instead and he finds his way into them, leaning over me carefully to avoid my stomach. He smells like exhaust fumes and sweat, but he's here. I hold him tightly to me, kissing his cheek before I let him go. "Sorry I'm late," he says.

"You better be sorry." I narrow my eyes at him but I can't hold onto an angry expression for very long. I'm so overwhelmed with happiness that he showed up, and there's no way I could be mad at him.

Jessica takes up the ultrasound wand again and places it on my stomach. I'm just about to tell Jace about the rude woman in the waiting room and how I wish he could have been there to make me look better, when Jessica makes a curious sound. Her eyes squint as she stops moving the thing on my stomach, holding it precisely in place while peers at the computer screen.

"What is it?" I ask, my voice dry and panicky. Oh God, she's found something wrong with my baby. I grab Jace's arm. Jessica looks at me and then at Jace and starts laughing.

"No, no," she says, rolling her eyes. "There's nothing to worry about. It's just…" She turns the flat screen monitor toward us and points to the black and white image of our baby. My heart leaps into my throat. There on the screen, is a tiny baby hand. Jessica points to it with the computer mouse. "See there? Your baby looks like it's making a peace sign. There's a fist with two fingers open." She clicks something and the computer prints out a still image of the baby's hand. "I just thought it was cute. Your baby might be a hippie!"

"Nah," Jace says, squeezing my hand. "You know what that is?" He makes the same peace-sign shape with his hand, only he holds it out in front of him with his palm facing down. "That's a two finger clutch move. He's clutching an imaginary dirt bike."

Of course Jace would think about dirt bikes instead of peace signs. Motocross is his entire world, besides me. Jessica lifts an eyebrow. "He?"

Jace shrugs sheepishly. "Well, I was just guessing."

"Would you two like to know the sex of the baby?" Jessica asks.

I look at Jace, expecting to see him nodding impatiently. We've already talked about this and hell yes we want to know the baby's sex. But when I look away from the ultrasound screen, I don't see Jace looking excited like I had expected. He's...he's crying.

"Babe?" I ask.

He swallows and blinks back his tears. "Yes, Bay?"

"Are you okay?" I ask.

He nods. "Yep. I just...there's a baby in there." He runs a hand through his hair and looks at me like I'm the only person in the world. And for a moment, I feel like that's true. "I mean I knew there was a baby in there, but now I see it. It just hit me that I'm going to be a dad and that this is real and..." He sighs and a single tear rolls down his cheek. "I don't know, I'm just really happy with my life right now."

"Aww," Jessica croons. She fans herself with one hand. "So what will it be, Dad? Do you want to know your baby's sex?"

Jace glances at me for confirmation. Now I'm the one nodding impatiently. He gives Jessica the go ahead and she points to another place on the monitor. "Okay Mom and Dad... you guys are having a little boy."

CHAPTER 5

The next twenty four hours are one of the most amazing times of my life. They're amazing not because of what we do, but because of what we don't do. Jace doesn't go to work, I don't do any housework or baby planning or wedding planning. We don't talk about the future and we don't mention anything stressful for the entire day.

Here's what we do: Sleep in until noon, cuddle and talk about our favorite memories over the last year, make love, sleep some more, order pizza and watch movies.

It is a glorious day of relaxation. I have never been so in love.

And then, just like that, the sun rises again the next morning and Jace is up at the butt-crack of dawn. He tries so hard to be quiet as he tiptoes around our bedroom, trying to get dressed and brush his teeth without waking me up. But it never works. The moment he crawls out of our bed, I wake up instantly. It's like my body knows when he's not near me, no matter how long I've been sleeping.

Jace slips into the closet and searches for clothes to

wear by the light of his cell phone. I yawn and stretch my arms above my head, twisting and sprawling until I'm taking up the entire bed. Jace's pillow smells like him so I nuzzle against it until the ache of wanting him right next to me becomes overwhelming.

"You're weird," he teases as he pads across the room in his bare feet. I look up from the pillow just in time to see him pull off the shirt he slept in and toss it at my head. It covers my eyes, blinding me but I don't mind one bit because the shirt smells like him. Like boy and body wash and home.

"So are you," I tease back as I roll over and squeeze his shirt to my chest. "You're the weirdest."

He leans over me on the bed, bracing himself against the headboard as he kisses the top of my head. "I love you," he says. "Try to have some fun today."

"How could I possibly have fun when you're going to be gone all day?" It's Thursday and Thursdays are Jace's busiest training day. He's usually giving lessons at the track until eight or nine at night. I used to go with him but ever since the morning sickness set in, I've been staying home more and more, trading in the bleachers for my bed. Today will definitely be one of those days.

"Do I know your schedule better than you do?" Jace says, poking me in the nose. I swat his hand away and think about his question. "What do you mean? I don't have a schedule...I'm just a fat preggo with no job and no school until after this kid is born."

"You are so not fat," he says, leaning over and kissing me on the forehead and then the lips. "But you're wrong. Becca is coming over today. It says it on your online calendar. It's a good thing we started using that thing because now one of us can remember stuff."

"Is it Friday already?" I practically jump out of bed

with excitement before I remember how early it is and fall back down into the soft mattress. I rub my eyes and admire Jace's ridiculously hot backside as he pulls on a Mixon Motocross Park shirt and then buckles his black leather belt.

I let out a squeal of excitement. "Oh my God, I'm so excited to see her."

I can't believe it's finally Friday and my best friend is coming to spend the weekend with us. Becca and I grew up as best friends in my hometown. But now she lives an hour away since I moved to Mixon with Jace, so now our friendship is mostly texts, Facebook posts and the random meet up at a mall that's halfway between both of our houses.

"I love you," Jace says. Right about now, I realize he's been talking for the last few seconds but I wasn't paying attention to any of it. I was trying to remember all the things Becca and I planned to do in the emails we exchanged while planning for this weekend. "I love you, too." I say quickly. I grab his hand and pull him back onto the bed with me and kiss him like I'll never see him again. He smiles and trails a hand down my cheek. "I gotta go, babe. You get some more sleep and call me when you wake up."

THE APARTMENT IS SO BORING WHEN JACE IS AT WORK AND I'm pacing around like a weirdo, anxious and excited for my best friend to get here. According to my online calendar, which I checked because I was too embarrassed to call Becca and ask because then she'd know I forgot, Becca is supposed to get here around ten in the morning. We planned a big day of wedding planning, gossip, and eating junk food.

I'm getting a start on the day by baking half a dozen

apple turnovers, using my mom's recipe. They're actually so easy to make that a kid could do it, but Jace and Becca practically worship me when I make them, so I keep the recipe a secret in order to preserve my perceived baking skills.

While they're in the oven making the kitchen smell amazing, I start making a dish of seven layer dip for us to snack on after lunch. It always tastes better if it's made in advance and refrigerated for a few hours, but I'm so tempted to eat it now. Stupid pregnancy cravings.

We call it seven layer dip because it started out having seven layers when my mom used to make it for holidays and parties. But she included things like salsa, jalapenos and these weird yellow peppers that Becca and I can't eat no matter how hard we tried. When we were old enough, we dove into the kitchen unsupervised and created the greatest layered chip dip known to man: a bottom layer of refried beans, a thin layer of grated cheese—sharp cheddar, hand grated only, another layer of thinly sliced avocados, then sour cream, then more cheese, then a final top layer of sliced black olives. So it's technically six layers but some-times we add extra cheese layers to make a legit seven layer dip.

I sprinkle on the final layer of black olives, swallow back my urge to eat the entire dish at once, then cover it with plastic wrap and toss it in the refrigerator before I change my mind.

My phone buzzes and I wash the cheese and avocado from my hands before checking it. My heart hurts when I read the message. This can't be good.

Becca: Hey Bay, I have some bad news…

My fingers shake as I type out a reply. Bad news can only mean one thing - she's canceling our weekend plans. I bet she got called into work or something. Ugh. Now tears form in my eyes and I try to blink them away and remind myself that I'm an adult and adults don't cry over broken plans.

Me: What is it?

Her reply takes forever. Like, literally, one entire forever goes by before she replies and in that forever, I open the refrigerator door and contemplate eating the seven layer dip before my apple turnovers come out of the oven. Hell, I could eat both of them back to back. It still wouldn't heal over the pain of not getting to plan the wedding with my best friend.

My phone buzzes. I close the refrigerator door, blink back more tears and tell myself to stop being so selfish. Maybe something terrible happened to her and that's why she can't come over. With fresh new fears in my mind, I open her text message.

Becca: The bad news is that you're gonna have to get off your preggo ass in a minute…

My eyebrows draw together. **Me:** Huh???

Before I can press send, there's a knock at my front door. My phone buzzes again.

Becca: BECAUSE YOUR BEST FRIEND IS HERE, BEYOTCH.

With a squeal, I sprint through the kitchen, almost tripping on the shiny tile flooring in my fuzzy socks. I yank open the door without even checking to make sure there's no murderer on the other side. Luckily, it's just Becca. She's been keeping up with her hair highlights and now her hair is so long it's almost down to her butt. We both do this little jumping up and down while squealing thing and then I throw my arms around her in a hug.

"I cannot believe you tricked me like that! You're such a jerk!"

She makes this coy look and then says all innocently, "I don't know what you're talking about…"

"I was seriously going to cry when I thought you weren't coming," I say. She laughs and takes off her backpack, setting it on the floor in the foyer. "I have some more things," she says, popping back outside. When she returns, she's carrying a large duffel bag and a black sign that's as big as a poster board for a school project, but it doesn't look like a homemade display board.

"What's this?" I ask, taking the sign and turning it around. It's black foam board with white lettering that has obviously been professionally printed. It only takes a second to recognize it as a type of sign they use for motocross races, only…it's not a real sign. This one says MAIN EVENT in big letters and then under that is the date of our wedding, August 9th.

Becca bursts into a big smile and scrolls through her phone, looking for something. "It's your wedding announcement sign! Isn't it awesome? My boss has a printing machine and he made it for me."

"I'm still confused," I say. But I smile anyway because her excitement is rubbing off on me.

"Well you know how you wanted the wedding to be kind of motocross themed?" she says. I nod and she finally finds what she was looking for on her phone. She turns it toward me and it's open to an image that she had saved from a screenshot. "I got the idea off of Pinterest. My friend Kristina pinned it to her motocross board and I thought it was so perfectly cute and so perfectly you."

The image shows a girl standing on a dirt bike track, holding up the sign as if she were starting a real race. Behind her is a guy on a dirt bike, looking like he's ready to start the race. "This is really awesome," I say, immediately picturing all the ways Jace and I could take a photo on the track. "This will make an awesome picture for the wedding announcement and the invitations and, like everything. Did you bring your-?"

Before I can finish my question, Becca pulls a massive camera out of her oversized purse. "Camera? Yep."

At the moment, I am super glad that Jace isn't here because he always rolls his eyes when I start to squee like a crazy girl, because that's exactly what I do. "This is going to be amazing!" I say, bouncing on my heels. "I know I make fun of you for your Pinterest obsession, but this time it totally paid off."

She bats her eyelashes and waves her hand at me. "I know, I know," she says. "Being a loser who spends all weekend on the computer instead of going on dates has finally come in handy for once."

"Aww," I say, frowning. "Are you doing okay? You're still totally over Braedon, right?"

She nods. "Yeah, we're cool. We're totally better off as just friends, but it's not him that I miss. I miss having a boyfriend. Someone to text me good morning and someone to hold my hand and all that..." She stares at somewhere off in the distance and sighs. "Oh well," she says, perking up again. "This weekend is about *you*, my dear. Not me."

I feel a twinge of guilt for being in such a happy relationship when Becca is so single it hurts. She's such a great person and she deserves someone to care for her. I don't know why she can't ever find a good guy. Of course, our hometown totally sucks when it comes to guys. If not for meeting Jace at my grandparent's house in Salt Gap, Texas, I'd probably still be single as well.

"Actually..." I begin, remembering my conversation with Jace the other day. I know he thinks it'd be a bad idea to try and hook up Becca with his best man, but that doesn't mean they can't just flirt with each other until he goes back to California, right? Becca lifts an eyebrow for me to continue. We sit on the couch and I prop the main event sign against the wall. "Okay, so, this isn't a big deal at all, okay? Like it's so far from a big deal that it's not even a deal at all…"

Becca rolls her eyes. "Then why bother telling me?"

"Because Jace's best man is totally hot and I think you two would look super cute in pictures together."

Her eyes narrow. "Why just pictures?"

"Well…because he lives in California so he'll only be here for the wedding. But Jace says he's an awesome guy, so the good news is that you'll have someone to hang out with for all the planning and festivities."

She laughs. "How hot is this guy?"

"Hot. Like Jace hot."

"Is he into motocross?"

"Yep. He's semi-pro and races all over the country."

"Badass." Her eyes drift off into secret Becca daydream land. After a few moments she says, "Well I guess having a hot guy to flirt with for a few days is better than having no guys to flirt with for a few days."

"Your time will come, I promise. One of these days, we'll be planning your wedding."

"And maybe your baby could be my ring bearer!"

"How'd you know it's a–?" The words are out of my mouth before I can realize what I'm saying. I slap my hand over my mouth and Becca's eyes go wide. Even though I wanted to know the baby's sex as soon as possible, Becca wanted to wait. She said it would be more fun that way.

"You're having a boy!?" She grabs my hands and squeezes them tightly. "Oh my God, a little boy? I'm so excited I can't even think straight."

I hang my head, not wanting to admit it but knowing I can't deny it. "I'm sorry I accidentally ruined it for you."

"No way, are you kidding? I'm so excited! He's going to be a little Jace!" Becca stands up from the couch and begins pacing the living room, ticking off ideas on her fingers. "I'm going to throw you a dirt bike themed baby shower, and we can get you all checkerboard and motocross patterned baby blankets and...do you have a name picked out yet?"

I shrug, lacing my fingers together in my lap. "Nope. No names, no plans. I'm kind of on the verge of a panic attack about it all." I don't even realize I'm playing with my engagement ring until Becca's hand falls over mine. She looks me in the eyes, giving me a reassuring smile. "We'll focus on the wedding first and then the baby. It's all going to be fine." She points her finger at me as if she's my mother. "Absolutely no worrying. I forbid it."

"Yes ma'am," I say sarcastically. She punches me in the arm. "Okay," I say, grabbing my wedding planning notebook off the coffee table. So far, it's a whole lot more notebook than wedding plans. But I plan on resolving that soon. "Let's plan this wedding!"

Becca holds up an identical notebook that she bought to match mine. She calls it her Bridesmaid planner. She slaps her notebook to mine as if we're holding champagne glasses and making a toast. "Let the planning begin!"

CHAPTER 6

"I really think I should be driving," Becca says after a particularly annoying driver cut in front of me on the highway and I had to slam on the brakes.

"I'm a good driver," I say, rolling my eyes. "That idiot is just a bad driver."

"Should pregnant people be driving? I think I should drive." Becca eyes my steering wheel as if by pure willpower alone, she can make it lift out of my hands and move over to her side of my car.

"I'm *fine*," I say for the millionth time on this car trip. I'm tempted to slam on the brakes again just to mess with her, but Jace would kill me if he saw me treating my car badly. He's always going on and on about taking care of the engine and what not. And since he is technically my mechanic, I should listen to him. I glance in my rearview mirror, hoping to see his truck behind me on the road. It's no surprise that all the cars behind me aren't him.

After Becca had made that comment about my son being her future ring bearer, I realized that I would need a ring bearer as well. So as soon as I called my mom to tell her about my plan to ask my ten-year-old brother Bentley to be in my wedding, she insisted that we meet up so I can ask him in person.

It sounds legitimate enough, but I'm not fooled. I think she's just trying to look for any excuse to hang out with me. She doesn't really admit it, but I know she misses me since I moved out. And although we used to butt heads all time, now things are different. I've gotten older and she's become more laid back. She and David eloped recently and she's never been happier. She's cool. I never ever thought I would say that about my mom, but it's true. My mother is cool.

We agreed to meet up at the Woodberry Mall which is the halfway point between Lawson and Mixon and home of the awesome smoothie place. Since Jace was at work, he said he'd meet us there as soon as he gets finished. So he's probably an hour away for all I know, but I can't stop looking into my mirror, hoping I'll see him on the road.

Gosh, I'm a freaking lovesick lunatic.

"Do you think it's natural to be so in love with someone that all you do is think about them constantly?"

"Where'd that come from?" Becca asks, looking up from her cell phone.

I shrug. "Just wondering if I'm crazy for missing Jace all the damn time. Seriously, I miss him every time he's gone. Sometimes I miss him when he's getting ready for work because it means he's *about* to be gone. Something is wrong with me. I should be an independent woman and all that..."

Becca shakes her head. "Nothing is wrong with you, Bay. You're in love. That's a good thing. Now, are you trying to get a speeding ticket, or are you so in love with Jace that you can't realize you're going ten over the limit?"

· · ·

Mom waves her smoothie at us as we approach the smoothie shop. Bentley is deeply involved with his Nintendo DS so he doesn't even notice us arrive. Mom hugs me, squeezing me so close to her that I can smell her shampoo. It's a different brand than the kind we used when I lived there. Probably because Mom never cared about that kind of thing and always grabbed the cheapest stuff on the shelf, whereas I have to have the silky and sleek shampoo, otherwise my hair is an awful fuzzball.

Becca and I order smoothies. Green tea for her and angel food cake for me. Hey, I'm pregnant, okay? I deserve this. Mom slides over closer to the wall when I approach so I sit by her and Becca takes a spot near Bentley, who, for all I know, still hasn't noticed our arrival.

"How was the drive?" she asks, leaning forward in her seat. We're in a corner booth at the front of the shop. It has an excellent view of the sidewalk so I should be able to see Jace the second he gets here.

"Mom, you act like it's some kind of three day road trip or something. It's just an hour."

She rolls her eyes. "That's still a long drive. I'm just making sure you're okay."

It is so weird how things are between us now. It's almost like we're...friends. Becca sips on her smoothie and nudges Bentley in the shoulder. He looks up from his game and his expression goes from mildly annoyed to bashful in about two seconds. He's only ten years old, but it's obvious he has a crush on Becca.

"Bayleigh has something to ask you," Becca says, winking at him. He looks at me expectantly. I shake my head. "No, I can't ask until Jace gets here. I don't want him to miss out."

"Jace is coming?" His wide eyes sparkle with anticipation at this news. I nod and he bursts into a grin. "Awesome."

My brother is one of the only people I know who loves Jace just because he's a great guy and not because he's a famous motocross racer. There are a ton of cool things about my fiancé's fame, but a major downside is that he can't really know who is his friend because they truly like him or if they just want to rub elbows with someone who makes them look cool. Jace always says he has three people he can trust: his mom, me and Park. Then last Christmas when he spent the entire holiday break with my family, he added Bentley to that short list of trustworthy people after, on the fifth day of Bentley being completely obsessed with how cool Jace is, somebody asked Jace for his autograph at the mall and my brother asked why.

Once Jace realized Bentley knew nothing about professional motocross and only liked him because of who he was as a person, my adorable little brother got added to the list.

Sometimes I wonder if Jace would have still dated me or even been friends with me if I had known who he was when we first met. Somehow, I doubt it. But the feeling makes me ache in all sorts of ways so I put the idea out of my mind and focus on my family.

"So what's been up, Mom? Where's David?"

"He's working," she says with a sigh that doesn't sound like she's upset about it. She still smiles when she talks about him which lets me know that their love is still running strong. "But enough about us, Bayleigh. How's the wedding planning?"

I shrug and Becca's jaw drops to the floor. "Bay! Don't just shrug like it's nothing! We've put a lot of work into this wedding already," she says to my mom. "Bayleigh has her dress and we have the engagement photos scheduled for tomorrow and she's pretty sure she wants a cupcake cake, and—"

"Cupcake cake?" Mom asks, lifting an eyebrow. "Like a cake that's shaped like a cupcake?"

Becca and I exchange glances. Mom is clearly not on Pinterest, or even remotely in touch with modern times. I try to explain it to her while Becca jumps on her phone to pull up her Pinterest app.

"It's like a bunch of cupcakes that are arranged on a tiered stand to look like the shape of a regular wedding cake. We can't decide on square or circular, but I think I like square the best."

"Are they all squished together to make a cake?" Mom asks. It's all I can do not to laugh. Luckily, Becca has the image pulled up on her phone now. She shows it to my mom. "Ahh," she says, nodding. "That looks awesome! Are you going to do pink icing like that?"

"No, I was thinking purple and turquoise as the wedding colors," I say. "Like maybe alternating each cupcake with a different color."

"Or swirling the icing colors together!" Becca says.

"That would look awesome!" I say, imagining fluffy icing in deep purple and turquoise colors swirled together.

"What would look awesome?" We all look up to see Jace standing at our booth, double chocolate smoothie in his hand. I stand up so hard I bump my knees on the table and promptly collapse back into the booth.

"When did you get here?" I ask. Mom quickly follows my question with one of her own. "How on earth did you have time to get a smoothie without us noticing?"

He slides into the booth next to me and Mom, placing a quick kiss on my cheek before answering. "Ya'll were pretty involved in whatever you're talking about. I waved but no one saw me."

"We're talking about cakes shaped like cupcakes," Bentley says.

Jace nods as if that doesn't sound completely weird. "I don't see why we can't just have a wedding cake shaped like a life-sized dirt bike."

"Jace Adams," I say with a pretend sigh. "Everything is not about dirt bikes!"

"Uh, yeah it is," he says, sticking out his tongue at me. Bentley lifts his hand and Jace fists bumps it as if they're a part of this secret boy world that only the two of them understand. All the women at the table roll their eyes.

"Boys…" Becca says.

"So I have a question to ask my favorite little brother," I say.

"I'm your only little brother," Bentley shoots back.

"And that means you're the one who gets this great honor," I say, holding my hand to my chest. "Will you be my ring bearer?"

He's silent for a beat and then he looks from me to Jace. His bottom lip slips under his teeth and he sits there, looking a little confused. "A ring bearer is the boy who brings the ring down the aisle in a wedding," I explain. "You'll get to hold the rings on a pillow or something and bring them to us. You'll be a part of the wedding."

Jace drums his fingers on the table. "What's wrong, little dude?"

Bentley stares at the table. "I thought the ring bearer was for babies. Aren't I too old for it?"

My heart sinks. My brother doesn't want to be in my wedding. And worse, he's insulted that I offered him a so-called baby role. It takes me a minute to realize that not only is Jace talking, but he doesn't even sound concerned. "Nah, dude," he says. "Ring bearers just have to be younger than the bride, but there's no age limit for it.

Besides, the rings are very expensive and I don't trust anyone but you to carry them, so I was really hoping you could do me this favor."

Bentley's demeanor changes instantly. He looks up from the table and looks at Jace. "Okay. I can do it."

"Really?" I say, feeling a little less anxious. "Are you sure? It would mean a lot to me."

He nods. "Yeah, I'll do it. Do I get to wear a suit?"

"Totally," Jace says before I can answer. "You can come pick one out when I get mine."

My brother's little eyes light up. "Cool! Mom, will you take me?"

Mom's eyes sweep to the left and she stares into the distance as if she's trying to visualize her schedule to see when she can take him. Jace shakes his head. "I'll come get you. You can ride with me and my best man. We'll get matching suits and we'll look badass." He holds up a hand and Bentley slaps him a high five.

I sip my angel food smoothie and stare up at Jace as he smiles and chats with my brother. He is the greatest man on earth and for some crazy reason, he's mine. I love how he can turn any situation into a good one without even batting an eye. It's like his brain never developed the part that makes you freak out. I hope our kid inherits his ability to stay calm and solve problems logically. I hope our kid inherits everything about him.

CHAPTER 7

Becca, in her ever growing fears of having some kind of gluten allergy, spends the rest of the day lying on my couch complaining of stomach pains. It really puts a damper on our shopping and wedding prep plans, but I don't complain because I know she feels bad enough and she doesn't need to feel even worse about it.

"So what exactly is wrong with you?" I tilt my head and look at her from my place on the couch's armrest. "You don't look sick."

She grabs her stomach. "My stomach hurts. It's hard to explain...it's like it just hurts but it's a different type of hurt than a regular stomach ache."

"Can I do anything for you?"

She shakes her head. "I'm sorry for ruining our day. I'll be better in like five hours so maybe we can do something tonight?"

"Sure," I say, tossing a couch pillow at her. The sound of Jace's house key shoving into the lock startles me. He's not normally home so early. I rush over and pull open the door for him. He's smiling and practically bouncing on the balls of his feet.

I poke him in the stomach. "What's going on with you, mister happy face?"

"I had two clients cancel," he says. "I'm glad you're home. I was thinking I could take all of us out for dinner? Becca?" His eyebrows furrow when he sees her clenching her stomach and wincing in pain.

"I'm sick," she says. "Ya'll go without me."

"Are you sure?" Jace asks at the same time I say, "No way. I'm not leaving you."

She waves her hand at me. "No, ya'll go. Have fun. Seriously!" She smiles. "You have prime cable here, so I'm all set."

I roll my eyes, hand her the remote control and give her a hug. "Alright, Jace. Where are we going?"

Perry's Steakhouse is an upscale restaurant that was probably designed for entertaining celebrities and not normal people like us. Of course, one person in my relationship can actually be considered a celebrity, and he's standing next to me acting as if this isn't scary.

We're waiting in line at the hostess station behind two middle-aged couples. Their outfits alone probably cost more than my car. And here I am in a pair of dark wash skinny jeans, flats I bought from Payless and a navy blue sweater. Jace wears jeans too, but he makes them look fancy just by being himself. He's wearing a black button up shirt with the sleeves rolled up to just below his elbows, showing off his muscular forearms. Only they can't be seen right now because he's also wearing his black leather jacket, which I am completely and totally in love with.

I tug at the zipper of Jace's jacket. "Why did you insist on coming here again? We don't fit in here."

"Because you've never had a volcano," he whispers, leaning down so I can hear him. This volcano better be as great as he says it is, because we drove an hour to get to this place and now I'm feeling totally awkward about it. I swear people are staring at us. And besides, since when is Jace so ridiculously excited about desserts?

We move forward one place in line and it occurs me for the first time that I have no idea why Jace likes the volcano dessert at Perry's Steakhouse. He started talking about it a few days ago when I was making a bowl of ice cream and covered it with enough chocolate syrup to drown a small village. He had said that this restaurant had the greatest dessert in the world and that as soon as he had a break from work, he was going to take me.

A sick feeling climbs up into my throat as we reach the hostess stand and Jace requests a table for two. How many times has he done this before? With other girls? Is the Perry's Steakhouse volcano dessert his way to impress other dates?

And if so, why did it take him over a year to bring me here?

The hostess smiles and greets us the way she greeted everyone before us, so I guess that's a good sign. It's not like she recognized Jace and asked him what happened to his other girlfriends... I roll my eyes despite myself as she takes us to our seat. Of course that wouldn't happen. That kind of stuff only happens in movies. In all reality, this is a fancy place with respect for its guests so even if she did recognize him, even if he came in here every other week with a new woman on his arm, she probably wouldn't have said anything at all. Ugh, sometimes I really over think things.

Jace lifts an eyebrow as he sits across from me at our table. I realize he's been talking this whole time and I hadn't heard a word of it. I smile and nod, hoping that's a satisfactory answer.

"Were you even listening?"

"Mhm." I take a sip of water and look over my menu, which is flocked with gold print on a velveteen paper. Jace gives me a look that says he's not buying it. "So you're perfectly fine with postponing the wedding until next year?"

"Totally," I say as I skim the list of appetizers, not knowing what half of those fancy dishes actually are. "Wait." I look up as realization of what he just said comes to me a little later than it probably should have. "You're postponing the wedding?"

Jace bursts out laughing. He points his finger at me. "I knew you weren't listening."

I hit him with my menu, but you know, in a quiet way that doesn't draw any attention to me. "You almost gave me a heart attack."

"Well you're giving me a heart attack by not paying attention. What's going on in that mind of yours?"

I shake my head. "Nothing."

"It is so not nothing."

I can't tell him that I've been obsessively wondering how many other girls he's brought here. Jace is a pretty understanding guy and he's put up with my crazy fears for over a year now, but I can't possibly tell him this. So I take the easy way out and smile. "It's nothing, Jace. I'm just a little overwhelmed with all the wedding stuff."

"Well don't be. It's supposed to be fun."

I blink and take another sip of my water. Holy crap, I can't believe he bought that. Jace's ability to read me like a book has taken a huge step backward. Or maybe I've just gotten better at hiding my insane insecurities. I'm feeling proud of myself as I look over the menu, trying to find something to order that I both know how to pronounce and would like to eat. I know there's a smug smile on my face, but I don't care.

"I think I'll order the coconut shrimp," I say a few moments later. "With….sweet potato fries? And ranch to dip them in."

"You are the weirdest," Jace says with that little adoring smile he gets when he thinks I'm doing something weird but not so weird that it creeps him out. "Oh, you're not off the hook, by the way. I'm going to find out what's actually bothering you. I'll just wait until after dinner."

I roll my eyes, keeping my face calm and my tone serene. "You're cute, Jace. But I'm fine. You're thinking way too much here." I shake my head like I just can't believe how silly he's being and then go back to the menu. "I guess I'll stick with the coconut shrimp. It's hard to choose since I haven't been here before. I guess it's easier for you because you've been here a million times though."

If my voice had any hint of disdain in it, I didn't mean it. Or...maybe I did. Jace shakes his head. "I've only been here twice, and both times I got the steak, so I'm sticking with it this time as well."

Twice. So only two girls... or possibly one girl two times. Ugh, I can't believe I'm still worrying about this. Jace is with me and that's all that matters. I've been his one and only girlfriend for the last year and two months and that's what I should focus on when thinking of us. Not the fact that he had other girlfriends before me. "Wait, you've only lived here for one year," I say. Immediately, I snap my mouth shut because I did not mean to say that revelation out loud. Jace's eyebrow is probably permanently cocked in an expression of confusion by now. "Yes…" he says, sliding his finger down the soft edge of the menu. "What does that have to do with anything?"

"You've only lived here a year and Perry's Steakhouse doesn't exist in California where you lived before you met me." It's all starting to make sense in a weird way that doesn't make sense at all.

"So, what's your point?" Jace asks. "You wondering why I came here twice since I've known you?"

My heart thumps beneath my chest. "Well...yeah."

He leans back against the smooth leather bench seat behind him, crossing his arms in front of his chest. "You could have just asked me, sweetheart."

My face flushes and I gnaw on my bottom lip, suddenly wishing the waitress would come take our order. But of course, she is nowhere to be seen. Two other couples sit at tables around us and I glance at them with their sweet expressions and their enthusiasm for being with each other and suddenly I feel like a huge jerk. "You're right," I say, folding up my menu and folding my hands on top of it. "It's stupid of me to care. I was just being...hormonal, I guess."

Jace stares at me with those piercing but gorgeous eyes of his. "Mr. Fisher brought me here when we talked about the opportunity for me to come work with him at Mixon Motocross Park," Jace says. "And then Park and I came here last year during that weekend where you and Becca were having a girls only night to study for the SATs. Do you remember that? I remember calling you from Park's rental car when we were driving home and I talked about the volcano so much you had joked that I should marry it instead of you."

I laugh. "I totally remember that. You were obsessing over that stupid dessert."

Jace laces his fingers through mine from across the

table and leans forward, his eyes serious. "It is a dessert worth obsessing over," he whispers.

"You are such a dork," I whisper back.

He shrugs. "Takes one to know one."

After we've eaten dinner, our waitress comes to check on us and Jace orders the volcano. Her eyes light up and she surveys us in a new light. "Are you dining here for a special occasion tonight?"

"No," I say, right at the same time Jace says, "Yes." I look at him waiting for an explanation. He extends out his hand toward me and tells the waitress, "This is my fiancé's first time here and she's never had the volcano."

This makes the waitress laugh because she had been obviously expecting a better reason than that. "You're in for a treat! I'll be right back."

I'm expecting her to bring us the infamous desert, but she doesn't. Instead, she arrives with a rolling cart that looks like an ultra-fancy stove with just one burner on it. There's a shiny metal wok-shaped pan on top of the stove. On the fold out arm of the stove cart is a massive oddly shaped bowl of ice cream. She fires up the gas burner and the blue flames glow beautifully in the darkened restaurant. I watch in awe as she pours syrup and sugar and other ingredients I don't quite see clearly into the pan and cooks them over the burner. An instant aroma of brown sugar fills the air and makes my mouth water. I only thought I was stuffed full from dinner- now I am desperate for this ice cream.

She takes the bowl of ice cream and stabs a few decorative pieces of chocolate lace into the sides of it. Then, with careful precision, she lifts the pan off the stove and pours the sugary concoction on top of the ice cream. She places the bowl in the center of our table, and then takes a lighter out of her apron. It's the kind of lighter with a long barrel. "Enjoy," she says with a smile before clicking on the lighter and touching it to the top of or dessert. A quick burst of blue flames erupts on top of the ice cream, caramelizing it for just an instant before the fire burns out.

My mouth has been open wide and childlike for a few minutes now. I finally remember to close it when Jace says, "Told you it was awesome."

We grab our spoons and dive in. I know I'm a pregnant chick right now, so pretty much anything with sugar in it is something my brain absolutely loves, but this volcano is the most amazing thing I've ever eaten, hands down.

"Oh my God," I moan between bites. "This is so good."

Jace nods. "I...told...you…" he says, his mouth full. He dives in to grab another spoonful but I knock his spoon with mine. "Back off, mister. Pregnant chick gets twice as much since she's eating for two."

He relents and lets me scoop up the best possible bite out of the whole bowl–it is equal parts ice cream and caramelized, gooey delicious brown sugar. "You're such a gentleman," I tease him.

He smiles. "You're lucky you're so damn cute."

"DINNER WAS SERIOUSLY THE MOST AMAZING THING EVER," I say as I slide my hand under Jace's elbow and hold on to him as we leave the restaurant. It's warm outside but I hug him close to me anyhow. I love the feeling of holding onto his arm when we're walking. We could be anywhere in the world and it would still feel like I'm home if I'm holding onto him. "Thank you for taking me."

"You're quite welcome," he says, stopping to hold open

the door for an older couple who has just arrived at Perry's Steakhouse. I step aside and let them in, and then hurry to catch up with Jace.

Jace lifts his arm slightly and I grab onto it again. "Would you like to do anything else tonight? There's a mall not far from here."

"I don't think anything could make this day any better," I say. "It's pretty much perfect the way it is. I say we go home and watch movies."

"Perfect, eh?" He tilts his head to look at me, his eyes an expression of challenge.

"Yes it was," I say. "Don't try to think up some way to make it more perfect because it won't happen. This day was absolutely perfect and nothing can ruin it."

Jace clears his throat. His arm stiffens under my grip. It doesn't click right away that his arm is stiffening for a particular reason. Nope, I'm still blissfully walking along the cobblestone walkway in front of the restaurant, heading toward Jace's truck and thinking all kinds of things about how perfect everything is.

"The hell are you doing here?"

I look up and find Ian standing perfectly still a few feet ahead of us. Jace steps forward, his arm holding me back just a few inches. My stomach twists into a knot and sheer panic flits across my body. The strong repugnant scent of Ian's cologne triggers an outpouring of memories, all the weeks we spent together when I was constantly around the scent of Ian's cologne.

Well...this night was perfect, I think.

Right before I lurch forward and throw up.

CHAPTER 8

The volcano does not taste as good when it's coming back up. Luckily, in my nauseated daze, I had leaned over a bunch of bushes and now, after a few moments of hurling, all of the food and puke nastiness is pretty much hidden under a mass of green foliage. I'm vaguely aware of Jace's voice saying something, and then Ian says something back, in a less friendly voice.

A hand touches my back when I stand back up. Jace leans toward me and I close my mouth, hoping to God that he can't smell my puke breath.

"Are you okay?" he asks. His eyes stare into mine as if we're the only two people on earth, but I know better. I nod and clench my teeth together. I know Ian is still standing around watching this scene and I don't want to talk to him. I don't want to see him and I definitely don't want to smell his cologne. He was the worst part of who I am. And he's in the past. He does not define me now.

"Move along," I hear Jace say. I know he's talking to Ian but I refuse to look up and acknowledge him myself. I'm perfectly happy staring at my black velvet flats. I am going to be the bigger person here. I'll stay silent and go on with my day. I will not give him the satisfaction of talking to him.

"So it is true," Ian says. "Bayleigh did get herself knocked up."

"Who the hell told you that?" Okay, I screwed up on this whole staying silent thing.

Ian wears crisp black slacks and a black button up long sleeved shirt, complete with a tie. He looks exactly like the servers in restaurant. He must have finally decided to get an honest job.

He looks me up and down and I cringe when his eyes linger on my stomach for longer than necessary. Although I am pregnant, I'm wearing a loose-fitting shirt and you can't really tell from looking at me. But Ian remembers the skinnier me from two years ago. He can probably tell that my stomach is bigger from a mile away.

"Who told me?" he says with a snort. "Everyone. The whole damn town knows you got yourself knocked up and then left town so you wouldn't be embarrassed about it."

I see red. "Screw you, Ian. That is not what happened and you're a dumbass if you want to believe gossip."

He grins as if we're playing a game and he just won. "Sure as hell looks like what happened."

I feel Jace's hand press against my back. "You're done," he says. His voice is serious and deep and for a split second, I think he's talking to me. But when I look at him, his jaw is rigid and he's staring straight at Ian. "Get out of our way. I'm sure you have some tables to bus or floors to mop."

"Man, screw you." Ian snarls. He stands up straighter, shifting from one foot to the other. He wants Jace to do something. He wants a fight, a scene. Because that's the kind of person he is.

But Jace is better than that. I know it.

I'm gently pulled to the side and a few moments later, we've walked right around Ian. Just like that. As if it wasn't a big deal. I draw in a deep breath and slowly let it out. I will not glance back. I will not try to have the last word. He's just not worth it.

I do a pretty good job of holding it together as we walk to Jace's truck. But the moment he closes the passenger door for me, I burst into soft tears. I turn to the right and pretend to be really interested in looking out of the window, hoping that I can get it together and stop crying before Jace notices. We pull onto the highway and a warm hand touches my thigh. This kind of comforting touch is always his way to let me know he's aware that I'm upset but isn't going to push me to talk about it. I know he means well, but I ignore him. I don't want to talk. I don't even want to look at him.

I spend the long drive home staring out of the window, watching the trees and buildings and cars zoom across the glass. The only thing I can think about is how, yeah, Ian might be a total asshole, but he is right about one thing. I am a girl who got knocked up and then moved away from her hometown. I can dress it up as much as I want—I can say I'm engaged and I'm in love and pretend that I totally planned life to happen like it did, but that's not true. My pregnancy was an accident, plain and simple.

Sure, we're happy about it but we're also terrified. At least, I'm terrified. I don't know how to be a mother. My mom and Becca's mom assured me that motherhood would come naturally to me and that I'd be great at nurturing this baby when he finally arrives. But I'm not sure how much of that is the truth or just their hopeful wishing. Aside from my happy relationship with Jace, I've never been good at anything in my life. What have I accomplished besides graduating high school with all the other students in my class?

Not a damn thing.

I didn't even pay for my own dinner tonight. Nor my wedding dress, or anything else I use in this life. I am completely worthless and a total drain on Jace's life and finances. He could be working more if it wasn't for me always wanting him to take a day or two off to hang out with me. He'd have a ton of money if he didn't pay my doctor bills and buy me stuff all the time. And he wouldn't be tied down to a life of being with me and our child if I had never entered his life and, in Ian's words, *got myself knocked up.*

I was supposed to go to college and get a job working at Mixon Motocross Park with Jace. But now that I'm pregnant, he suggested that I wait until our baby is a few years old before I start working. Jace doesn't want me to be stressed out and wants me to relax. Well how can a girl relax when she just realized she's completely worthless and a failure at everything?

CHAPTER 9

I had hoped a good night's sleep would wash away all of the pain and turmoil from last night's run in with Ian. But all of that hoping and praying was in vain because as soon as Jace's alarm goes off in the morning, I wake up, stare at the ceiling and become overwhelmed with feelings of hopelessness.

And as much as I don't want to admit it to myself, seeing Ian after so long away from him brought back some awful memories. Not memories of happiness or longing, that's for damn sure, but memories of that summer I spent away from home. Ian was the reason I had gotten grounded and sent away to stay with my grandparents for three months. He was the selfish prick who begged me to send him a dirty photo from my cell phone and I was the idiot who went along with it.

I was so stupid back then. I can't believe I used to like Ian. Like, *really* like him. I thought about him nonstop and I doodled his name in my notebook like some kind of teenage airhead. All of that pathetic adoration was completely unfounded because Ian didn't do anything to deserve it. It wasn't romantic or charming. He treated me like shit and somehow that made me want to try even harder to make him like me.

I always had to message him first and he would take forever to reply. He never wanted to talk about my day or listen to my thoughts about things I cared about. He just wanted to hook up and when we couldn't hook up due to my curfew, or Mom being too strict, all he wanted to do was talk about hooking up. As much as I wish I could go back in time and stop myself from ever dating him in the first place, I can't. And I wouldn't even if I could, because Ian getting me grounded was what led me to meet Jace.

The bed shifts as Jace sits on the edge of the mattress to put on his shoes. "Do you love me?" I ask, my voice raspy from a night of sleep.

"With all of my heart," he says.

I roll over and bury my head in the pillow. "Good," I murmur as I feel the pull of sleep take over. "I love you, too."

AT A MUCH MORE MANAGEABLE HOUR OF THE MORNING, after Jace has left for work, I finally wake up and find my best friend happy and looking less poisoned from gluten on the couch. She grasps a cup of hot cocoa in her hands.

"Ooohh, I want some," I say, eyeing the steam rising off her mug.

She nods her head toward the kitchen. "I've got the Keurig all set up for you. Just press the button."

I rush over and press the button, smiling when I see she's chosen the ugliest mug in the cabinet for me. This mug was a gag gift from her to me when I moved in with Jace a few months ago. "Every home needs an ugly mug," she had said. "Just to remind you where you came from."

It is big and heavy and has an ugly Christmas sweater type print all around it. Pixelated reindeer shapes and big green and red faux-stitching letters that read Happy Holidays. You can still see the twenty-five cent thrift store price tag written in permanent marker on the bottom because that stuff does not come off in the dishwasher.

Becca chops up a basket of strawberries, separating them into two piles for the both of us. I pour sugar on top of my pile and she rolls her eyes at me. "That kind of defeats the purpose of having a healthy breakfast."

I poke out my stomach as far as it'll go and pat it with confidence. "Yeah, well I am eating for two and at least one of us wants sugar on these strawberries."

We eat and watch trashy reality television and everything is fun and happy for about five minutes. Then, from out of nowhere like some kind of emotional punch to the gut, I remember last night. Ian and the way he made me feel. The things he made me think.

"You okay?" Becca asks. I nod and put on my best smile. It seems to work because she goes back to watching the TV. I'm tempted to tell her all about it. If I do, I know she'll launch into a verbal counter attack, calling Ian every bad name in the book and then telling me everything I want to hear. Things like how I'm not a shitty person and how I shouldn't let him get to me because he's an idiot and I am a great person.

If I told her about my emotional pain right now, she would hug me and make it all better. But I keep my mouth shut. I'm not sure if I'm ready to let all of this go and pretend like I'm not a massive embarrassment to myself and a disappointment to Jace. I'm not sure if I deserve to be comforted by a well-meaning best friend right now.

. . .

THE SUNNYSIDE BAKERY IS A SMALL STANDALONE BUILDING on the outskirts of Mixon. It looks like it used to be a Victorian style home, but over the years it was painted a pale yellow and transformed into a bakery. There are other bakeries in town and it might have been smart to sample all of them before deciding, but Sunnyside Bakery came highly recommended by Molly, who is the wife of Mr. Fisher at Mixon Motocross Park. I would be insane not to trust her opinion. Plus, I didn't trust my waistline if I had sampled from more than one bakery.

"Oh my God, this place smells so good," Becca croons as we get out of her car. She closes her eyes and breathes in deeply. "I think I just gained five pounds by smelling the air."

I wish I could share in her weight-gain-by-inhalation, but the smell of sugary foods just makes me nauseous at the moment.

There aren't any other people inside when we enter the bakery, but soft music plays from a speaker somewhere in the ceiling and the scent of freshly baked pastries lets us know someone is probably in the back.

"Are you sure she was expecting us?" I ask. Becca, ever the most perfect maid of honor, had called ahead and made us an appointment.

Becca nods. "Yep. Stop worrying."

Luckily, I don't have to worry. A plump woman with dark black hair emerges from the back room, patting her hands on the front of her pink apron. The name Carol is emblazoned on the top in curly letters made of rhine-stones. "Hello there!" she says, waving at us from the other side of the counter. "Are you my two o'clock?"

"Yes, ma'am," I say, stepping forward and shaking her hand from across the glass countertop. Dozens of beautifully decorated sweet treats beckon to me from beneath the glass. "I'm Bayleigh."

"So nice to meet you," she says, turning to my best friend. "And, Becca, right?" Becca nods and shakes her hand. I'm not sure what Becca had told her when she first made our appointment, but I'm eternally grateful for the soft way Carol smiles at us and how she treats us like real customers. I guess in the back of my mind I had been afraid that I'd be treated with judgment for being so young. I shove my hands into the pockets of my zippered hoody. It isn't cold outside–in fact it's shorts and sandals weather as evidenced by my sparkly pink flip-flops and cut off jean shorts. I just couldn't stop myself from wearing the hoody because it allows me to do exactly what I'm doing now: shove my hands in the pockets, zip up the bottom half and walk around covering my ever-growing belly. You know, just in case she doesn't know. Just in case some people don't know.

Carol seats us at a table in the center of the bakery and dashes off to retrieve our samples. I'm not sure what Becca has set up for us today because a week ago when she had called to ask about it, I was in the middle of a morning sickness puke session and had told her to use her best judgment because at that exact moment, I didn't give a damn.

Becca gnaws on her bottom lip as she sits across from me. "What is it?" I ask. "You're not supposed to be more nervous than I am, you know."

She chuckles. "I just hope you like the colors and the flavors and stuff."

"I'll like whatever you choose, I promise. You know me really well."

Carol emerges from the back room and Becca draws in a deep breath. I want to roll my eyes at how irrationally silly she's being, but I don't because I freak out about the dumbest things as well. Carol sets a white cake box on the table in front of us. "How many other bakeries have you tried?" she asks, sliding her finger under the cardboard flap to open up the box.

"None," I say. "Molly Fisher said we should come here so we did."

Carol beams. "Oh, Molly is the sweetest thing ever. Well, I hope you girls enjoy! What we have here is a sample of the double chocolate cupcakes and the French vanilla cupcakes. I told Becca you'd probably want both flavors so your guests could choose."

I nod. "Sounds good to me." Carol continues talking about the natural ingredients and special flavors she uses, and still hasn't fully opened the cake box yet, so we can't see inside at the creations that wait for us, and I lean forward, anticipation taking over my whole body. And then I see something on the box that makes me forget all about the cupcakes.

The paper order slip taped to the side of the box reads: *Adams, Jace and Bayleigh.*

Chills dance across my body. Carol's handwriting is a beautiful script and I love the way she swooped the cursive J and B of our names. But what I love more than anything is the way our names look together.

Bayleigh Adams.

That's going to be me in a just a few weeks. I blink back tears that can only be explained as crazy Pregnant Person Emotions and go back to being excited about the cupcakes. Carol has been talking this whole time, but I hadn't heard a word of it. Also, there's two plates in front of Becca and me, along with a fork. I hadn't noticed those arrive, either.

I tear my eyes away from my name on the paper and look for the cupcakes.

"Have you decided on a color yet?" Carol asks as she pulls two cupcakes from the box. "Becca and I discussed purple and turquoise but she wasn't sure if you'd like light colors or dark, so I made both."

Becca and I practically start drooling as Carol gives us each a cupcake with lavender icing swirled high. Next, she gives us its pastel blue equivalent. They're both wrapped in silver foil cupcake papers and have a light sparkly sheen on the icing.

"Beautiful," I say, picking up my fork but feeling like there's no way I'll be able to stab it into such an elegant creation.

Next, Carol takes out two more cupcakes for Becca and me. Only these have a deep rich coloring to the icing. A turquoise-blue and purple that is so stunningly beautiful that I instantly say, "This one! This color. Oh my God, it's perfect."

Carol and Becca laugh at my reaction but I don't care. I sit back in my chair and clap my hands in front of my mouth. "They are so perfect! So beautiful."

Instantly I can imagine my entire wedding–the flowers, the decorations, the invitations. Turquoise and purple. Weeks of being indecisive and unsure about everything now fold into one perfect moment where I feel that this wedding will be a breeze. It will be turquoise and purple and it'll be beautiful and wonderful.

"Bayleigh!" I look up to see Becca leap off her chair and come to my side of the table. "You're crying!"

Carol hands me a napkin, which is also purple, and I take it and dab my eyes and start doing this laugh-cry thing because I'm so emotional I can't help it. "I'm fine," I say after a moment. "It's just all so perfect."

"I'm flattered, darling," Carol says, sliding the plate closer to me. "But you haven't even tried them yet!"

Despite my natural instinct to keep something so beautiful intact, Becca and I dive into our cupcakes and it is immediately evident that we should have both double chocolate and French vanilla flavors at my wedding. We make it easy by requesting the chocolate ones to have turquoise icing and the vanilla to have the purple icing.

It becomes very clear that Becca and I only halfway know what we're doing when we decide we want to reserve these cupcakes for the wedding and Carol asks a question we hadn't even thought of.

"How many cupcakes will you be needing?" Her pen hovers over the order slip and my lips squish to the side of my mouth.

"Um," I say, looking at Becca. "We don't exactly know yet."

"A general rule of thumb is to order as many servings as people you are inviting, plus a dozen just in case. It's always better to have leftovers than to come up short."

"Yeah, that's a good idea," I say, feeling my cheeks turn red because I am a total idiot who doesn't deserve to plan a wedding if I am this stupid about it. "But I'm not even sure how many people we're inviting." I lower my forehead into my palm and stare at the floor. "I can't believe we didn't think of this," I mutter, so embarrassed that I never want to look up and meet Carol's eyes again.

Becca shuffles through her oversized purse and produces a small pink notebook. The one she calls her Bridesmaid Planner. I know I've made fun of that thing, but I am so glad she has it now. "We're inviting forty-three people. So I guess we should order about five dozen?"

"Perfect," Carol says, penning the number onto the order sheet. "Would you like these picked up or delivered?"

"Delivered, please," I say, grateful for a question that I

can actually answer. Well, sort of. "Becca will have to give you the address because it's some huge secret from me."

"Really?" Carol asks, intrigue dancing across her eyes. "The wedding location is a secret from the bride? That's a first."

I nod. "It's kind of a long story."

Carol relaxes in her chair. "I have plenty of time."

I glance at Becca and she nods encouragingly. Tiny butterflies fill my stomach as I prepare to tell them the story about my wedding location. It's not that I'm nervous or anything, it's just that every time I think about that night I get butterflies. I take a deep breath. "It was the day after Jace proposed and we were both super excited about the engagement, so we spent all day talking about the wedding. We knew we wanted it to happen as soon as possible because," I pause, not wanting to say the real reason. I'm not sure if Carol knows I am pregnant or not, and just in case she doesn't, I'd rather her not know. I swallow and continue, choosing my words carefully. "Because we've already been together for a long time and most of that time was long distance and we just really want to be married. We didn't want to wait. So, that was in May, and we choose August ninth to get married just because it felt like the quickest time we could get married while still having enough time to plan a wedding. Then, it was like two in the morning and I had spent all night searching online for the perfect place for the wedding. I wanted somewhere beautiful but it couldn't be far away because my family and friends can't exactly afford plane tickets and hotel expenses just to come to the wedding, so it had to be in Texas. There are like no pretty places in Texas, by the way."

This makes Carol laugh. Maybe she thinks I'm joking, but I'm not. "So anyway, I was freaking out about trying to find a place that's both small and beautiful and not too commercial and a place that kind of feels like home. Like the perfect place to marry someone. And Jace, meanwhile, hadn't been helping me at all. He was playing Xbox all night and just nodding when I'd show him stuff online. Then, when I was really discouraged about it, he suddenly sits up and drops the Xbox controller and is like 'Oh my God, I've got it. I know the perfect place!' So I asked him where and he just shook his head like a big jerk and said it was so perfect that it would have to be a secret. He said it'll be better that way."

Carol's eyes light up and Becca smiles devilishly because she already knows the answer to Carol's next question. "Well, where is it?" Carol asks her in a fake whisper. Becca pretends to zip her lips closed. "I'll write it down for you but I can't say it in front of Bayleigh."

I roll my eyes and don't even try to hide my goofy smile. I have to admit that not knowing the location of my own wedding until the day it happens is kind of awesome. Carol excuses herself to the back so she can put in the details of our order and Becca and I dive into the rest of our cupcakes.

My phone vibrates and I take it out of my pocket to find a text from Jace.

Jace: Still doing stuff with Becca?

Me: Yup!

Jace: Mind if I hang out at the track and ride a bit?

Me: Of course not. Have fun, babe. I love you.

Jace: ILY more!!

When I look up from my phone, Becca is staring at me. "What?" I say, shoving it back into my pocket. She just shakes her head. "*What?*" I say again, only this time it's not a question but more of an annoyed remark.

"You always get that goofy smile when you're texting

Jace," she says. I can tell instantly if you're talking to him or someone else by the way you look at the phone."

"So what? I can tell when your mom texts you because you look pissed off," I retort.

Becca groans. "Tell me about it. One of these days I'll make enough money to move out and be on my own like you. That will probably take forever, though."

I lick the remaining icing off my plastic fork and then point it at her. "Or you could find yourself a rich boyfriend. Preferably a motocross guy like Jace." My eyes light up. "Ooh! Or his friend Park! He's probably rich since he's semi-pro. You need to meet him, marry him and then be my best friend-slash-motocross wife bestie forever!"

She sighs. "If only life were that easy…"

I sigh, too, but for a different reason. "You never know," I say. And it's true. You really *never* know what life will bring you. Even when you think you've got it all figured out, you're wrong. And then, months later, when you think you really do have control of your life, you're even more wrong than you were the first time.

That's not always a bad thing. There have been times in my life where I felt that every single decision I had made was wrong and detrimentally stupid. But then somehow, everything works out. I've screwed up way more than Becca ever has, and yet here I am with Jace and a happy life and a future family. I can't imagine what kind of great things will happen to Becca when it's her time to find true love.

While we're saying our goodbyes to Carol, she takes my hand and squeezes it. "I love that you aren't doing everything strictly by the book," she says, smiling. "I can't think of a better way to start a marriage than by doing things your own way."

For some reason–okay, it's probably the hormones–I

feel myself tearing up at her kind words. "Thank you." I turn away quickly so I won't have time to let the fresh tears fall down my face. Today is a good day, I remind myself. There's no reason to let crazy hormones jump in and ruin it.

Becca lowers the volume of her car stereo at exactly the wrong moment. Taylor Swift just belted out the loudest part of the song, and unfortunately, so did I. I slap my hand over my mouth and slump lower into the passenger seat. "You can warn a girl next time you're going to do that," I mutter, but I doubt she hears it over her maniacal laughter.

"Okay, okay," she says, after laughing so hard she almost started crying. "I actually turned off the song for a reason. We need to plan your wedding announcement photo before I go home. That way I have time to edit the photos and have some printed so we can design the invitations."

"Good idea." My phone buzzes and I notice Jace's name flashing across the screen, but I let it ring so I'm not rudely interrupting my conversation with Becca. "Mr. Fisher won't mind if we use the track and we still have a few hours of daylight. Think we could do it today? Jace is probably still in his gear so he'll already be dressed. I need to do something about my hair and makeup though."

My phone stops ringing and then starts back up a moment later. I glance at the screen. It's Jace again. "Go on," Becca says, taking one hand off the steering wheel to motion for me to answer the phone. "Don't make your sweetie pie wait forever."

"Helloo-ooo," I sing into the phone. I hope Jace isn't

too worn out from riding to want to take photos with me this afternoon.

"Is this Bayleigh?"

My heart stops cold. The voice on the other end of the line is not my fiancé. "Hello?" he says. "Bayleigh?"

"This is Bayleigh." The words don't even sound like they're coming out of my mouth. "Who is this? Why are you on Jace's phone?"

"Bayleigh, it's Bobby. From the track."

Chills. Fear. I don't know what comes first. Bobby isn't just from the track. He's the on staff as a full time paramedic. He's the guy who's always hanging out next to the ambulance, watching the races and diving into action when someone gets hurt.

"What's going on? Where's Jace? Why are you on Jace's phone?" A million other panicked questions flow through my mind but I'm too choked up to get any of them out.

There's shuffling on the line and I can hear road noise and movement on the other side. The next three seconds of silence are the longest of my life. Becca watches me with worry, her eyes flickering from me to the road and back.

He takes a deep breath. I can hear the sirens of an ambulance burst to life in the background. I'm going to throw up and this time it won't be from the hormones.

Bobby's words are slow and carefully chosen. "I'm taking Jace to St. Mary's. You need to come quick."

All of the background noise disappears. "Is he okay?" I ask, knowing as I say the words that I won't get an answer. Bobby has already ended the phone call.

CHAPTER 10

After fifteen minutes of agony and begging my best friend to drive more than ten miles over the speed limit, Becca pulls into the u-shaped emergency room driveway. I throw open the passenger door before her car comes to a complete stop. "Meet me inside," I call out before slamming the door closed. My feet feel numb as I run through the automatic glass doors.

I've never been to St. Mary's Hospital before and the overwhelming emotions flowing through me makes it hard to figure out where I'm going. A maze of beige chairs line both sides of the aisle, some with people and most of them empty. I wander through the chairs of the massive room, looking around for a sign that will tell me where to go.

The triage desk is to my left, after three rows of chairs and two massive potted plants. My heart thuds in my chest. By some miracle, I'm not crying. Shaking and stumbling over my own feet, yes. But not crying. I will not allow myself to cry.

I stop just short of crashing into the triage counter and the nurse on duty doesn't even look up at me. "Hello," I say loudly to get her attention. This is a freaking emergency room. People come here for emergencies and this woman needs to do her job. My head could be hanging onto my spine by a thread for all she knows, but she doesn't know because she's not *looking at me*. "Hey! I need help."

She looks up from her computer screen, her expression unfazed by my yelling.

"Fill this out," she says, sliding a clipboard toward me. I shake my head. "I'm not here to check in. I'm here to see my fiancé. He was just taken here by ambulance."

"What's his name?"

"Jace Adams."

She types something into the computer. I peek over her shoulder at the area behind her that leads into the rest of the hospital, but I can't see anything. My phone sits silently in my fist. I haven't stopped looking at it, wishing and hoping that Jace would call me, tell me he's fine and that he just broke his pinky or something. "You need to take a seat," the nurse tells me. "We'll notify you when there's information."

"What!" It is not a question. "What the hell does that mean? I'm not going to take a seat. I need to know his status right now. I need to be back there with him."

"Have a seat please. We'll be with you shortly."

"You've got to be kidding me!" I kick the potted plant next to me but with its enormity, it just sits there, unaffected. "Jace could be dying right now and I need to be there. I need to be with him."

Her eyes narrow. "You will see him when the doctor approves it but if you continue to be disruptive, you'll be escorted out of the building."

My back straightens. She might be glaring at me as if she's won this round, but I have too much at stake to keep bitching about it. "Fine," I mutter, turning around. I choose a chair closest to the wide double doors that lead into the emergency patient rooms and sit, only to stand back up two seconds later. I can't sit at a time like this. I check my phone again. Pace. Try sitting and then stand back up. Pray. Look at my phone.

Becca appears at my side. It couldn't have been more than a few minutes since she found a place to park and walked inside, but it feels like it's been an eternity. I catch her up on what happened with the rude nurse and Becca snarls. "What a bitch."

"I can't do this," I tell her. My voice cracks but I blink back the tears and force them to stay put behind a wall that I can't possibly allow to break.

"Bayleigh!" I whirl around and find Ash Carter jogging across the emergency room, decked from head to toe in motocross riding gear. His boots drop dirt onto the shiny hospital floor. Ash is Mr. Fisher's son-in-law and one of Jace's good friends. His shoulder-length brown dreadlocks are pulled back in a ponytail.

"What happened to Jace?" I ask. Ash crashes into me, hugging me tightly. He smells like exhaust fumes and sweat. I appreciate the gesture, but I kind of just want to shove him off of me and demand that he tell me every detail right this freaking second. When he does pull away, his face is stricken with grief.

"He's going to be okay," Ash says, squeezing my arms.

I sigh. "Please tell me what happened. I haven't seen him. I don't know anything and it's driving me crazy."

Ash takes a deep breath. His eyebrows draw together, making me think for a terrifying second that he's not going to tell me what happened. "We were screwing around after practice because the track was closed so we were the only two people out there."

"And?" I fold my arms over my chest. He's deliberately taking longer than necessary to tell me what happened.

"And, well...we were freestyling a bit?" I don't know why it sounds like a question when he says it, but the guilt that falls over his tanned features tells me he's embarrassed to be admitting this to me.

"What exactly do you mean when you say *freestyling*?"

He stares at the floor. "We were doing tricks and stuff. Jumping over the ninety-foot finish line double."

"And he crashed?" I actually manage to say the words without bursting into tears. I've never seen Jace crash, exactly. I've seen him slide out in a shallow turn or bump into another bike at the starting line and lose his balance. He's never *crashed*. "How bad was it? Where did he crash?" My questions fly out a mile a minute, faster and more detailed with each time Ash doesn't answer. "Is he unconscious? Is his bike okay?"

The last one makes Ash laugh. He shakes his head. "His bike is toast. Probably needs a good three grand in repairs. Knowing Jace, he'll ditch it and buy a new one. And yeah...he's unconscious."

"Unconscious?!" My palms slam against Ash's chest. "You should have said that first!"

Becca calls my name and says things that mean nothing to me because I'm not listening. Oh, and those tears I held back earlier? They burst through my tear ducts like water through a broken dam. Dropping to my knees into the chair in front of me, I lay my forehead against the backrest and curl in on myself, kneeling backwards in the chair. Someone's hand pats my back while I cry massive embarrassing sobs.

I can't stop picturing Jace, my Jace, lying unconscious on a stretcher in the back of an ambulance. Is he awake yet? Will he wake up? Does he miss me as much as I miss him?

"Bayleigh, I know you're upset," Ash says, in what I assume is in the middle of a monologue he's been saying for the last few moments that I haven't been paying attention. "But getting knocked out on a dirt bike is pretty common. It's happened to me a dozen times and it's probably happened to Jace, too. He might have some broken bones, but he'll be fine."

I sit up and wipe the wall of tears off my face with the back of my hand. "Broken bones? Did you see him up close? Was he hurt? Did you see blood?" Again, images manifest in my mind of Jace's unconscious body, now covered in bodily trauma with severed bones sticking out of his arms and legs.

I catch the sounds of a whisper and turn toward Becca, who snaps her mouth shut and smiles at me. She was probably telling Ash to shut up and stop making things worse for my overactive imagination, but I glare at her anyway. Hell, I'll glare at everyone and everything until I'm sure that Jace is going to be okay.

IT REALLY SAYS A LOT ABOUT THE STRUCTURAL INTEGRITY of St. Mary's flooring when, after half an hour of pacing the small area in front of the emergency room doors, I haven't worn a hole through the tiles. My friend Hana is here now, snuggled next to Ash in one of the waiting room chairs. Becca has called her mom asking for prayers and I called my mom, but didn't get very far into the call before bursting into hysterical sobs.

I'm rounding past the stupid overgrown fern in the corner when the emergency room doors swing open. A nurse in baby blue scrubs with her hair in a severely tight bun on top of her head steps out and surveys the room. "Adams?"

"Me!" I shout, running over to her. "Is he okay?"

"He's awake," she says.

"Oh thank God." I swallow but it doesn't help to soothe my dry throat. "Can I see him?"

She nods. "Follow me."

CHAPTER 11

There's a digital clock on the wall of Jace's hospital room. Red LED lights blare the time at me the moment I open my eyes. It's two-sixteen in the morning. The light is off in here, but the heavy oversized door is cracked a bit and it lets in all the light from the hallway outside. Hospitals don't shut down when it's time to go to sleep.

I yawn and sit back, straightening my spine from the awkward way I had been sleeping. The plastic fake leather armchair in the corner of Jace's hospital room had sufficed as my pseudo bed. I had dragged it across the room, right up next to Jace's bed, carefully avoiding the wires and tubes that hung from various places on his body.

The doctor had informed me that Jace suffered a concussion. After extensive testing, they said the damage wasn't bad but it wasn't good. He'd need to stay for observation and make sure his brain didn't start swelling or something else—some kind of fancy medical term that made my stomach tighten. Instead of dwelling on what might happen, I had promised myself to stay calm and trust that everything would be okay. There's no way fate would take Jace away from me. Not now.

My right hand is wrapped tightly in his. It's sweaty and uncomfortable but I don't dare move. As much as I want Jace to wake up and talk and laugh and kiss me, the doctor said it's best that he gets some rest now. His body can heal better when he's sleeping, and I'll just have to wait.

I rearrange the flimsy pillows in my chair and try to get in a more comfortable position. I tuck my other arm under the lowered handrail on the side of the bed and rest my head on the mattress next to Jace's shoulder. My anxiety fades as I close my eyes and soon, sleep overtakes me.

WHEN I WAKE UP FOR THE SECOND TIME, IT'S BECAUSE A nurse walks into the room. She lifts an eyebrow when she sees how I'm positioned both in a chair and on Jace's bed. I sit up quickly and rub my eyes. I almost expect her to chastise me for how I was sleeping, but she doesn't say anything at first.

She checks Jace's monitors and taps something into a tablet. "Good morning," she says finally as she adjusts the IV bag and checks the time on her watch. "Breakfast hasn't been here yet?"

I shake my head. "I don't think so."

"Has he woken up this morning?"

I shake my head again. My hand is still interlocked with his, my hand sweat and his hand sweat merged into one sticky mess. Still, I don't want to let go. Jace's constant sleeping doesn't seem to bother her. She tells me she'll request an extra breakfast tray for me and then leaves before I have time to tell her that won't be necessary. I'm still so full of nervous energy that I'm not sure I could eat right now even if I had food in front of me. And hospital food? No thanks.

After what feels like hours, I turn on the television in the room and try to find something worth watching, but nothing takes my mind off of the situation. I want Jace to wake up so badly but I don't want to be the one who wakes him up. I want to be patient and allow him to sleep as long as he needs to. But…I might yawn a little loudly and make a big deal about standing up and repositioning myself next to him on the mattress.

It doesn't work.

Even when his cell phone blares to life on the table next to the bed, Jace sleeps soundly. I peek over at his phone, the top corner of which is lit up red to signal that the battery life is low. It's his mother calling, and honestly, I'm surprised she didn't call sooner. I glance over at Jace and when he hasn't woken up by the third ring, I take the phone and answer it.

I'd normally be a nervous wreck talking to his mom for the first time ever, but somehow I manage to say hello without my voice cracking.

"Hello?" She sounds confused at first and then her voice softens. "Is this Bayleigh? Or did my son develop a high-pitched voice?"

I smile, hoping it takes the nerves out of my voice. "It's Bayleigh. Jace is still sleeping."

"Really? I guess he didn't have work today?"

"Work?" The word suddenly has no meaning to me. "Why would he be—Wait, do you not know what happened last night?"

"I haven't heard from Jace in days, honey. Why, what's wrong?"

She called me honey the first time she's ever talked to me. That's kind of a huge deal, but I'll have time to be excited about that later. Right now I feel sick to my stomach over the fact that his own mother doesn't know he's admitted into the hospital. It was all my fault. I'm the fiancé. I'm his emergency contact. I should have been smart enough to call her but it never even crossed my mind. I spent all night worrying about Jace and never once worried about his family.

I swallow and try to think of the best way to give a mother scary news. "Well...first of all, he's okay. But he's in the hospital from wrecking his dirt bike yesterday."

"What?" she snaps as if I've just told her some juicy gossip instead of terrible news. "He better not have broken any bones right before the wedding! Oh, I'm gonna kill that boy if he did."

"No...no broken bones. Just a concussion and some scrapes and bruises."

"No brain swelling?" She asks the question as if it were as casual as asking what's for breakfast.

"No swelling."

"Good."

Jace hasn't stirred since I answered the phone. I decide to talk a little louder. "Do you want me to wake him up for you?"

"That won't be necessary, honey. I trust you're taking good care of him. I was just calling to invite you two to come over and see Gary and I next weekend. Do you think ya'll can make it?"

I almost blurt out *Who is Gary?* but before I put my foot in my mouth, I remember that's his dad's name. Plus there's a bigger situation at hand right now. His mother just invited us to come visit them in California. For the first time.

"Um, sure," I say without really thinking about it. "I

mean, assuming he's out of the hospital and feeling better and all that, I'm sure we can come over."

"Oh he'll be out of there by this afternoon," she says with a laugh. "You take care of him but if that boy tries milking it just for the attention, you better tell him to get off his ass and take care of himself, okay?"

"Okay." I can't believe she's taking this so lightly. Her son is in the hospital. *The hospital.* My mom would be freaking out if I were in the same position, but Jace's mom acts like it's no big deal. "I'll talk to him when he wakes up."

"Great," she says in the same cheerful tone she's had she's the beginning of our conversation. "Tell him Dad's credit card has a lot of miles on it so he won't need to buy plane tickets."

"Sounds good," I say.

"Okay, hun. Talk to you later!"

When I hang up Jace's phone, I stare at the home screen for a few seconds while I take it all in. I've just spoken to Jace's mother for the very first time since our relationship began. And it wasn't even that scary. She was really nice. I mean, he had always promised me that his mother was nice, but I guess I never believed it. And up until now, I had known that the first time I met them would be at our wedding, but I was trying to cover up the nervous feelings I had about that and try to focus on the wedding. Now we'll be meeting them before the big day.

We're going to be staying with them in California. At their house. Will they make us sleep in separate beds? Will his mom's niceness be just an act meant to lure me to their home where she'll then berate me for ruining her son's life? What if she meets me and doesn't like me and then demands that Jace call off the wedding?

A heavy sadness presses into my chest as I stare at

Jace's phone. His background is a picture of us at the motocross track, him in his gear and me in my homemade T-shirt that says: The Future Mrs. Adams.

I remember when that picture was taken. It was during spring break when I spent the week with Hana while our guys rode dirt bikes all day. We both made shirts like that, using a plain t-shirt and iron on glittery letters, only hers was about Ash, of course. I had had so much fun with Jace and my new motocross friends. It never occurred to me that my boyfriend's sport is a dangerous one. I spent that whole week hanging out at the track and making fun of Jace for how smelly he got after a day of riding in the hot Texas sun. I never once thought that one day I'd be sitting next to him in the hospital.

His phone beeps one last desperate cry to be plugged into a charger and then it dies. I frown. Bringing a charger is probably something I could have put on the list for Becca. After they let me see Jace and they gave him his own hospital room out of the emergency area, Becca had went back to our apartment and collected some items for me. Clothes, toothbrush, snacks and my tablet. The tablet's charger also worked on my cell phone. I didn't think to ask for Jace's charger as well.

"Hey beautiful." Jace's voice is groggy from sleep and probably the drugs in this IV bag. "Why do you look so sad?"

I smile as my heart explodes with happiness over hearing my fiancé's voice after what feels like years of not talking to him. I hold up his phone. "It's dead."

He shrugs. "You're here, so I don't care to talk to anyone else."

I set the phone on a nearby table and stand up, leaning over him to kiss his lips, his cheek and his forehead. "I'm glad you're alive," I whisper. Jace reaches up and grabs my face, pulling me down for another kiss. "Oh yeah?" he asks playfully. I nod. "Because now I'm going to kill you for making me worry."

He smiles. "I'm sorry, baby. I'm fine, though. They'll let me go home today."

I open my mouth to say something, but stop when Jace's demeanor turns...sneaky? Or...smoldering? "What is it?" I ask. He gives me this lazy smile and pulls at my arm, tugging me closer to him. "You look really hot right now," he whispers. "I want you."

"Oh my gosh," I say, rolling my eyes. "You are in the hospital and you're thinking about sex?"

He shrugs and makes this face like he can't help it. "I always want to do you," he says. "It's your fault."

I stand up and put my hands on my hips. "And why is it my fault?"

He reaches out and pokes me in the stomach. "Because you're so *prettyyyyy*."

With one twist of his hand, he grabs me around the waist and pulls me to him, and then draws me in for a kiss. We make out in a hungry, eager way, but it's not as satisfying as at home because now all I can focus on is being gentle so as not to rip out his IV, or touch any part of him that's been injured. His torso is covered by a hospital gown and the sheets, but the doctor had told me that he was pretty banged up. No internal injuries though, so that's a good thing. I groan and pull away from kissing him so I can look him in the eyes.

"I'm sorry to ruin the mood, but I have something to tell you."

Jace winces as he shifts to the right in his bed. He pats the now empty space, motioning for me to lie down next to him. Carefully, I snuggle into the space next to him and rest my head on his shoulder. I take a deep breath.

"Okay, now you're scaring me," he says. "What is it?"

I take another deep breath. "Your mom called. I answered your phone. It was before the battery died."

He laughs. "Okay, what's so bad about that? Wait...is everyone okay?"

"What?" I snap, looking back at him. "*You're* the one who's not okay, mister!"

"I'm fine, babe. I promise. Just have a headache, that's all. So what'd Mom want?"

"Well I told her you were in the hospital with a concussion, and she didn't even seem to care."

He nods. "That's my mother. She raised a motocross kid. We get hurt. That's what we do."

"Why does everyone think this isn't a big deal? You're in the freaking hospital!"

"I'm sorry, baby. I know this is hard on you." He kisses the top of my head and I close my eyes as we cuddle on the stiff hospital bed. "I didn't mean to scare you. I wasn't supposed to crash, obviously. But I'm sorry you had to go through this. I'll be okay, I promise."

"You're about to be a father, you know. I can't have you risking your life just to do what Ash called 'freestyle tricks' after work."

Jace stiffens. "Did he say what kind of freestyle?" I shake my head and he relaxes. "Good."

"What's that supposed to mean?" I ask.

"So what else did my mom want?" He's changing the subject and doing a terrible job of being casual about it, but I'm definitely not in the mood to grill him on his definition of freestyling.

"She wants us to come visit. Next week."

"That's a good idea," Jace says. "They should totally meet you before the wedding. Besides, now that I'm hurt,

Mr. Fisher will let me take a couple of weeks off work to recover. So it's perfect."

"I don't know about this," I say, feeling my stomach twist into knots.

"What's wrong?"

"It's your parents. I'm nervous…What if they don't like me?"

Jace waves away my worries with a casual flick of his hand. "You're insane. They're going to love you."

CHAPTER 12

When Jace is out of the hospital, we make a trip to the mall and purchase new luggage. I've never really had a proper suitcase, always opting to toss my stuff in a duffel bag or backpack when traveling, and Jace's old luggage was from his motocross days and reeked of dried sweat and exhaust. He chooses this Oakley brand bag on wheels to be his new suitcase and I pick something more girly. A pink suitcase dotted with sparkly silver stars. It has pink wheels and a shiny pink handle.

"You won't have to worry about spotting this at the baggage claim," Jace says once we get home and I'm fawning over it and all of its cool compartments. "I don't know," I say. "I think it might need more glitter."

Jace flips open his pocket knife and slices through the plastic tags that I was trying, but failing, to rip off with my hands. Then he cuts off the tags on his new bag as well. We plop them onto our bed and begin packing. Our return trip plane ticket is for three days after we arrive in California. Three whole days of hanging out with Jace's parents.

I'm not even sure my body can handle that amount of nervousness.

"What's bugging you?" Jace says as he swoops behind me in our shared closet, grabbing a few button up shirts off the hangers and tossing them over his shoulder. I shrug and flip through my clothes, unsure of what to bring. "I'm just nervous, that's all."

"There's nothing to be worried about. Unless you're scared of flying." His eyes go wide in this evil way. "Wait, are you scared of flying?"

"No," I snap, making sure I sound confident so he won't catch on that yeah, I'm a little scared of flying. But that fear is nothing compared to the gigantic ball of nerves that took up residence in my chest the moment his mother called and hasn't left since. "I'm scared of your parents."

Jace laughs so hard and so loud that I jump and then immediately fake punch him in the arm. "Stop laughing at me!"

"You're so adorable, Bay. I love you so much," he says between laughter. "You have absolutely nothing to worry about. My parents are cool. I promise."

I draw in a deep breath and let it out in a slow sigh. "I really hope you're right."

Choosing enough clothes to last for three nights and three days with the potential of changing outfits halfway through the day poses the toughest task I've had to do in weeks. Planning a wedding feels like a cakewalk compared to choosing what outfits you want to be seen wearing around your future in-laws.

Jace has his entire suitcase full and ready to go by the time I've finally chosen which outfits I think I *might* be taking with me. Guys have it so easy. They wear jeans and shirts and they can mix and match everything in their wardrobe. Plus Jace looks hot in everything. I have to do this delicate balance between something that looks nice but not like I'm trying too hard, and something that doesn't show off my growing stomach.

I stare into the full length mirror on the back of the closet door, turning sideways so I can see my profile. My stomach isn't huge by any means, but it's slowly getting bigger each day. There's a little pooch there that is slightly bigger than something I could play off as having just eaten a whole pizza by myself. I lift my shirt and rub my hands over the pooch, reminding myself there's a growing baby in there. It's insane, when you think about it. A baby. A real, live, human being will jump out of me in a few months' time. Well…okay, maybe not jump. But I hope it's quick, and I hope it doesn't hurt as badly as it looks like on the movies.

Jace leans against the doorway of the closet, watching me watch myself in the mirror. "I thought your stomach would get much bigger this far along," he says, turning his head sideways. "We're like, five months now, right?"

"Twenty three weeks. They go by weeks for whatever reason," I explain. "Too many things happen each week for it to be based on the month."

He eyes me in this appreciative way and suddenly I'm self-conscious. I turn away from the mirror, covering my belly with my hands.

A moment later, his hands slide over mine as he hugs me from behind. His mouth presses against my neck, trailing kisses down to my collarbone. "I love you, Bay." Chills wash over me when his breath tickles my skin. "I love you, Jace." My words are a whispered reply and it's all I can do to even speak coherently when he does this to me. His hands slide up my arms and then back down again, circling around my protruding stomach and then wandering back up to my breasts. He cups them and his lips linger on my neck just a moment longer than usual.

"What is it?" I ask, twisting around to see him better. His face is shadowed from the dim light in the closet, but the naughty way he smiles lets me know exactly what he's thinking.

"Your boobs get bigger every day," he says, wiggling his eyebrows. "I like it."

I roll my eyes. "You're such a pig."

His hands slide around my waist and tug me toward him. I press against his chest and take special care to make sure my boobs get squished in a way that makes the cleavage from my tank top look as sexy as possible. "I'm your pig," he says with that goofy grin of his that I love so much.

Fifteen minutes later, my suitcase holds exactly one pair of jeans and two pairs of pajamas. I guess that can be considered progress. Jace lies on his back on the bed, tossing the remote control from one hand to the other.

"So tell me about California." I toss a blue shirt at him and he catches it but drops the remote.

"What would you like to know?" he asks. He folds my shirt in half and then in half again, setting it inside my suitcase.

"Well, the only thing I know about California is that it's really big and full of celebrities. Also, I'm not packing that shirt," I say, taking out the blue shirt and tossing it on the bed.

"Why not? You look awesome in it." Jace refolds the shirt and puts it back in my suitcase. I think the words he meant was that I *used to* look awesome in it. Now the shimmery blue fabric that's meant to hang loose at the stomach fits tightly around my midsection, stretching the thin fabric and making it look awful. If I tell Jace this, he'll probably ask me to try it on to prove it to him and that is so not happening. So I just leave it in the suitcase. I'll bring more than enough shirts to ensure that I won't be wearing that one on our short trip. "So, California," I say again. "You grew up there and you never even talk about it."

"There's nothing worth saying," he says. "I had an average childhood...went to school and raced dirt bikes. My whole life was dirt bikes. Same as it is here."

"You were pro though. That had to be different. I mean, you're famous here in Texas so I bet you're really famous in California."

Jace shrugs. "I haven't raced on the west side in two years. No one cares about me anymore. And that's exactly how I want things to be."

"Why's that?"

He looks at me. "Because I want things to be here with you."

Warmth spreads through me when I hear his cheesy answer. I don't know if he really means that or if it's just something a guy says to his pregnant fiancé to make her feel better, but it makes me all emotionally gooey anyhow. I lay out three dresses on the bed and try to determine which one I should choose to bring along. Jace points to the middle one, a black knit dress with long sleeves and a plunging neckline. "Good call," I say, taking the dress and folding it neatly into the suitcase. Black is a slimming color and I desperately need all the slimming illusions I can get.

"Tell me about your parents."

This makes Jace laugh for some reason. I frown. "Why won't you talk about them? I need to know about them so I won't go in blindly. I need some topics I can talk about with them."

"They're going to love you, babe. They're simple people, I promise. Dad works hard and Mom...well she's a really good housewife. She works hard at...watching TV. And they aren't going to talk about themselves, you know."

"And what are they going to talk about?"

"You." He says it all matter-of-factly and I lift an eyebrow. "I'm not sure I like that idea," I say, feeling trepidation creep over me.

I hold up a few more shirts for Jace and let him choose his favorites. He picks all the shirts with low necklines and I try not to make fun of him for his love of my new big assets. Jace helps me fold the clothes we picked for our trip and I hang the discarded options back in the closet.

"Baby, I'm nervous," I admit to him when my suitcase is finally packed enough for three days and nights.

"I know. And I know there's probably nothing I can say to make you feel better."

I shake my head. "There isn't. I'm going to be freaking out about this the entire time, no matter what you say."

He smiles. "I think you're more nervous about meeting my parents than you are about the wedding."

I nod. "Totally."

I zip up the suitcase and Jace sets mine on the floor next to his. "I know what will take your mind off it," he says, stepping closer to me. I sit on the edge of the mattress and take his hands in mine, parting my knees so he can stand closer to me. "And what exactly is that?" I ask, giving him a coy smile.

He leans forward and kisses me, slowly at first but then deeper, faster. My hands slide up his chest and cling around his neck, holding on tightly when he crawls on the bed, pulling me underneath him.

He rests on his elbows, hovering over me and he smiles when I kiss him, moving all over his face to kiss every single part of it. When my lips find his again, I suck his bottom lip into mine, lightly grazing my teeth over it. He groans and presses into me, lighting me on fire. My back arches to meet him and I grind against him slowly, again and again.

"That's it," he groans, sliding his hands down my sides. He slips his fingers under my tank top and slides it up and over my head. He lowers himself over me again and kisses my neck, my collarbone, my chest. His voice is raspy, desperate. "I'm gonna make you forget every single one of your worries."

CHAPTER 13

I'm not sure what I was expecting when we landed in California. Okay, maybe I did know what I was expecting. Celebrities. Fancy rich people. Paparazzi at every turn. You know, typical California stereotypes, because apparently that's all I know about the state.

"Sacramento International Airport?" The disappointment in my voice is impossible to miss. Jace looks at me funny as he winds an arm around my back and guides me through the throngs of people on our way to baggage claim.

"Where did you think we were?" he asks.

"You know. LAX. The airport that's always on TMZ and stuff."

Jace snorts. "Sorry to break it to you, but my parents live in Sacramento, not Los Angeles."

I put on a fake pout, but soon realize that I'm not faking it at all. I really thought we'd be swimming in famous people by now. I mean, this is California.

"What's wrong?" Jace asks. The way he glides through the airport without even stopping to read the signs or look for directions is the sign of someone who flies a lot. Someone worldly and experienced. It makes me feel this mixture of embarrassment over my own sheltered life and admiration for my super sexy fiancé.

I stop and watch the massive turning baggage claim belt as it turns around slowly, carrying people's luggage until they come to take it. It really is just like in the movies. Jace nudges me with his elbow, letting me know he's still waiting on an answer. "I don't know...I just thought we'd see some famous people since we're in California."

He smiles. "The day isn't over yet."

THE EXHILARATION OF BEING IN A NEW PLACE COMES TO A screeching stop when we arrive at the waiting area. "What are we doing?" I ask, looking around as if there is something here I'm supposed to recognize. "Aren't we renting a car or something?"

Jace's nose wrinkles. "You have to be twenty-five years old to rent a car, babe."

"Oh." I feel like an idiot now. "I knew that, I swear I did," I say with a pathetic little laugh. "I can't wait until we're old enough to legally do everything there is to do."

Jace slings an arm around my shoulders and pulls me close to him. "I can wait."

"Really? Why? We're basically kids and it sucks."

He shakes his head. A mother with three unruly toddlers rushes by, yelling for the kids to slow down. "I don't want to be too old, too soon. I want to live our lives as long as we can, you know? See everything we can and do everything we want. That can't happen if time speeds up and we're older."

"Oh blah," I say, leaning my head against his shoulder. "You always say all of the right things."

His lips form a slight smile, but his gaze is fixed somewhere in the distance. "I think a lot. I'm always thinking about something, so by the time I say it, I've had time to work it out in my mind. *You*, on the other hand…" He kisses me on the tip of my nose. "You are always talking. I think you might actually say words before your brain even thinks them."

"Oh shut it," I say, even though he's right. Jace is naturally quiet and I'm naturally talkative. I've always thought it balances out nicely between the two of us, but maybe I'm wrong. "Does it bother you that I talk too much?"

"You don't talk too much," he says. "A lot. But not too much. Besides, I like your voice."

"You better like it," I say, joking around with him. "Hey, why are we-?" I stop mid-sentence as realization comes to me. "How are we getting out of here if we're not renting a car?"

"We're getting picked up. I thought I told you all of this?"

"I guess I forgot," I say. Trepidation fills me as I put together the pieces in my head. "Your parents are picking us up?"

"Yes ma'am," he says in a fake Texas accent.

I let out my breath in a long, slow sigh. This is not what I was expecting. For some reason, I had imagined we'd rent a car and then drive to their house and that way I would have enough time to compose myself for meeting his parents. I know it's technically not that big of a deal, but it feels like one. I'm meeting my fiancé's parents for the first time and I'm pregnant with his kid and I'm practically a kid myself. I guess if I prepare myself for the judgmental glares and snide remarks beforehand then it won't hurt as bad when they happen.

My fingernails dig into my palms and the inside of my

bottom lip feels raw. I've been chewing on it absentmindedly and now I can't stop.

"They're here," Jace says, looking around. "I can smell her."

I smell it too. The scent of vanilla cupcakes and coffee. Two seconds later, a woman with bright blonde hair bursts through the crowds of people, her bright red lipstick molded in a beaming smile. "Jace!" she squeals, rushing up to him with her arms open wide. She wraps him in a hug and even though he's over a foot taller than she is, she almost makes him look like a little kid again with the way she hugs him, swaying back and forth like she hasn't seen him in forever. And, that's kind of true.

I recognize her from the photos I've seen of her, but Jace's mom is much more vibrant in real life. She's bouncy and colorful and all smiles. As soon as she releases him from her bear hug, she sets her sights on me.

"Hi," I say, lifting my hand in a pathetic wave.

"Bayleigh, my dear!" I suck in a deep breath to prepare for her massive hug, and even with my expecting it, her embrace blows me away. She is somehow soft and motherly with the grip of a boa constrictor. She clings to me twice as long as she did with Jace. Up close she smells mostly like coffee, but in a good way–like I'm sitting in a beautiful coffee shop surrounded by books. When she ends the hug, she pulls back and holds me at arm's length, gripping my elbows so hard it hurts. "I am so happy to meet you."

"Me too," I stutter like some kind of idiot. "It's nice to meet you."

Her features are strikingly similar to Jace's now that I'm seeing her in person. She has a nice nose like he does and a strong jawline. Her eyes, though lined with fine wrinkles, sparkle the same way Jace's does when he's really excited about something.

"Where's Dad?" Jace asks her.

"He had to work," she says, curling up her nose. "You know how it is."

Jace nods and I just stand here, wearing a small smile and trying to look nice because I don't know how it is. I've never met the man. It feels like a small blessing in a way, that I only had to meet one of the parents this time. Now, when I meet his father later in the day, I would have had time to compose myself and think of something better to say, something impressive and something that would make you glad your son is marrying this girl.

MRS. ADAMS, OR JULIE, AS SHE INSISTED THAT I CALL HER, drives a massive SUV type vehicle called an Escalade. But I'd rather call it a tank because it's so huge. My butt slides across the tan leather backseat with every turn she makes. Jace turns around from the front seat and gives me a silly grin. "You okay back there?" he asks after a particularly sharp turn sent me flying.

"Yeah, yeah," I say. "Maybe I'm having fun back here."

"I could be having fun too if you'd have let me sit with you!"

"You haven't seen your mom in forever," I say in a snappy but joking voice. "You need to sit by her."

Julie nods appreciatively. "I like this girl," she says, looking back and winking at me. "I like her a lot."

They talk about Jace's job and our apartment and random other things that moms always ask about. When the conversation turns to dirt bikes, I accidentally tune it out and become amazed by the sights out of the window.

In Texas, the land is flat and dry and boring. There's cows as far as the eye can see. Here in Sacramento, the entire place is beautiful. Hills and mountains and beautiful homes. Even the air smells different. Or maybe that's just the new car smell from Julie's Escalade.

We come to a red light in a busy part of downtown. Jace turns around and slaps his hand on my thigh. "Hungry?"

"Starving. Are we almost there?"

"Oh, honey we're like an hour away," Julie says. "That's why we were thinking Mexican. You up for Mexican?"

"Huh?"

Jace laughs. "I told you she wasn't paying attention. Mexican food. Yay or nay?"

I rub my hand over my stomach. "Yay. Definitely yay."

WE VISIT AN ENORMOUS TWO-STORY MEXICAN RESTAURANT called Escalante's for lunch. Things are going really well and I'm feeling less nervous by the second. Sure, I still have to meet Mr. Adams, but if he's anything like Jace's mom, it won't be so bad. Now all I have to do is play it cool and be sweet and charming, not get any unexpected morning sickness for three days and then make it home without any incidents that would make them hate me. So far, so good.

"I am so excited that Jace found someone to make his life with," Julie says. I only halfway heard what she said because I was stuffing my face with the most delicious tortilla chips I've ever eaten. She smiles warmly and pats my arm from across the table.

"Me too," I reply quickly, because that answer sounds like it would fit in with whatever she had just said. Jace and his mom laugh. I glance over at Jace, lifting an eyebrow. He just winks at me and dunks another chip into salsa.

Julie lets go of my hand and squeezes Jace's hand this time. She's a very touchy person. "Bayleigh is such a sweet girl." She's telling her son this, but she looks over and smiles at me. "I was a nervous wreck when I met Gary's parents. Of course they were both strict and very religious and since I was already pregnant with you at the time, they acted like I was some kind of evil witch who had come to take their son to hell with me." She rolls her eyes. This story probably explains a lot about why she's so kind to me and in a weird way, I am grateful for Jace's mean grand-parents. And I know this is a terrible thing to think, but they've both been dead for a while now, so I won't have to meet them and be subjected to the same treatment as Julie went through.

Jace glances at me and then back at his mom. "I'm lucky to have you guys as parents," he says. It's probably the most intimate thing I've heard him tell another person besides me. "You always support me, and I'm really grateful for that."

Julie's face crinkles up and for a moment, it looks like she might cry. "I love you, Son."

Our waiter brings Julie a margarita and Jace makes a little whimper as if he wanted one too. "I'd get you one if you were at home," his mom says. "This place probably prefers not to break the law by selling alcohol to minors."

I laugh and use the opportunity to poke fun at Jace. "Can't rent a car...can't buy alcohol," shaking my head as if I'm disappointed in him. "Would you like to order off the child's menu?"

Jace's mouth falls open. He reaches toward me, grabs a strand of my hair and tugs it. "Did you just pull my hair?"

I ask, laughing. "Way to dispute the fact that you're not a kid!"

Jace laughs and sticks his tongue out at me. I stick my tongue right back out at him. A flash snaps both of us back to reality. We look over and find Julie holding up her phone and nodding. She just took a picture of us and now I'm so embarrassed I could die.

"You better delete that," Jace tells his mom, still laughing.

She shakes her head. "This is going right in the digital scrapbook. Trust me. When you're forty years old, I will send you this picture and you'll be really glad I took it."

"That's so far away," I say, letting my imagination take a hold of me. "We probably won't even remember what we looked like when we were this age."

Jace shakes his head and says something about how he will have stayed just as sexy as he is today, thanks to modern science and cryogenics or something like that. I take Julie's lead and smile at him, but my mind is really somewhere else, my thoughts lost to the possibilities of the future.

I had been looking at this all wrong. Meeting Jace's parents isn't just a one-time meet them, charm them, and never see them again thing. It's the start of a lifetime of knowing each other. Of holidays and birthdays and vacations to see their grandchild. It's two more people to call if Jace ends up in the hospital again. One day she really will show us that picture she just took. And we'll be older and greyer and our child will be in college. Maybe we'll have two kids. And she'll know all about it because she's family. Because we're family.

As terrifying as it is to meet the people who brought my soul mate to this earth, I now realize how important it is to know them.

CHAPTER 14

I always knew Jace came from a wealthy family, but I never knew *how* wealthy. When we arrive at his parent's house, I have to physically stop my jaw from hitting the floor by clenching my jaw together. We drive up the cobblestone driveway, which is U-shaped around a massive water fountain with a concrete angel in the middle. The landscaping around the front yard is so pristine, it most definitely has a gardener who tends to it daily.

Their house is a massive brick structure with tons of windows and a high peaked roof. There's two white columns that frame the doorway, rising from the ground up to the roof. It's right about now when I notice that the house seems so huge because it's not just a typical big two-story house. It's three stories.

Julie parks up front and turns down the radio volume before shutting off the engine. "Gary gets so annoyed when I leave the radio up loud," she explains, rolling her eyes as if he's a mean old man and she's the cool young kid who loves loud music.

I glance over at Jace to see his reaction to coming home

to such a massive place. He's just staring at his phone, checking the supercross results. He must sense me looking at him because he looks up, his eyes finding mine instantly. "Eight bedrooms," he says, nodding toward the house. "I'll let you pick which one we stay in."

"I thought we'd be staying in your old bedroom?"

He shakes his head. "That's been turned into the trophy room."

We climb out of the car and I follow Jace to the back of the vehicle even though I know he won't let me carry my own luggage. "Trophy room? Now I have to see this."

Julie laughs. "I wouldn't exactly call it a trophy room." She grabs Jace's suitcase and he takes mine, carrying it by the handle and not letting it roll.

"You know the foyer part of our apartment?" he asks. I nod. It's a teensy space between the doorway and the living room where we hang our keys and kick off our shoes. There's also about twenty random dirt bike trophies cluttering the area. Jace mostly teaches people how to ride these days, but occasionally he and Ash will drive a few hours out to race the pro class at a local track. "Pro" class doesn't mean the professional supercross racers that Jace was banned from before I met him. It just means people who aren't famous, who are just as fast and get to race for money. The terms are confusing, but I've just learned to accept them for what they are.

"My old bedroom is pretty much like that," he says, closing the car's cargo door.

We enter through the front door, which I'm assuming is for my benefit. The front door is, of course, two doors that swing open into a marble floored foyer that is seriously bigger than my living room at home.

A massive staircase is to the left, taking you up to the second floor balcony. Beyond that, I can just see where another staircase starts, going up to the third floor. It's all so shiny and beautiful that I'm scared to walk around out of fear that I'll dirty the place just by being in it.

Julie leads us up the stairs, which have carpeting so plush that it feels like I'm walking on a cloud, and then to the right and down a massive hallway. There are six doors in the hallway, and the square footage of the hall alone is probably more than my entire apartment back at home.

"Let's show her the 'trophy room', Jace." Julie makes air quotes around the last two words in a way that is clearly mocking him. She stops at the very last door on the right and motions for Jace to show me inside.

"Are you ready for this?" he says, lifting his eyebrows. "It's pretty epic in here."

I nod. "I'm definitely ready."

I'm picturing class curios lining the walls, carrying various trophies, plaques and ribbons. Maybe a framed picture of Jace holding a trophy. I know he's been racing dirt bikes since he was a kid, so there's probably pictures of him from all ages on the walls.

The first thing I see when I step into the room is gold and silver shiny plastic dirt bikes. A sea of trophies of all colors, many of them taller than I am, line the walls and the floor. I can only take one step inside the former bedroom without crashing into a wall of trophies that would undoubtedly crumple over like a pile of dominos. Every single space in the room holds a trophy. Hundreds of them. I was right about the plaques—the walls are filled with dozens of plaques shaped like a number plate, the number one in the center, and a brass tag at the bottom, telling which year he won the championship.

"Holy crap," I mutter under my breath. "I don't think this room is big enough."

"That's what the attic is for," Julie says. "Trust me, you do not want to see the attic."

"I can't believe you kept these," Jace says, shaking his head. To me, he says, "I quit caring about the trophies when I was twelve. I wouldn't even go pick them up after the race because I had so many but Mom insisted on getting them."

"Of course I wanted them," Julie says. "My son won them and I was proud." Her eyes light up a moment later. "Oh my god. Jace! I just remembered the greatest thing. We have to show her your first!" We shuffle back into the hallway and Jace mutters, "*Oh god*," under his breath. I have no idea what she's talking about but I am excited to see it if it makes Jace this embarrassed. Not many things embarrass him, so this should be good.

Back downstairs, through fancy entryways and around a spiral staircase in the kitchen that goes up to some mysterious level, Julie stops in the dinette. I had noticed a massive dining table in a formal dining room down the hall, but this room is just off the kitchen and has a round glass-top table with only four chairs. This must be where Julie and Gary eat their meals together when they're not entertaining.

The room overlooks the backyard which can been seen through floor to ceiling windows. There's a porch, tons of palm trees and tiki torches, a grass roofed hut that looks like a full bar, and then the most magnificent swimming pool I've ever seen.

There's a pool at my mom's house, but it's small and she rarely had the money to get the water cleaned so we could swim in it when I was a kid. Mostly it sat half-empty, with green water. Sometimes we'd get it ready for summer—those were always the best summers. Something tells me

Jace has never had to worry about their swimming pool's water going green.

I glance up at Jace and he slides an arm around me, a simple gesture of love, something he does automatically whenever I am around.

"Let's get this over with," he says. "Where is it?"

Julie's smile stretches from ear to ear as she walks across the small room, to where a few shelves line the walls in a random pattern. There, in the middle shelf, sits a framed picture of a little boy. Next to it is a trophy that's not even as tall as the picture frame. I walk up to it, studying the picture of what I know is my fiancé.

"This was Jace's very first race," Julie explains. "There were fifteen other kids in his class and he was so nervous and so excited."

The picture is slightly grainy from having been blown up larger than the standard size for photos back when we were kids. No doubt this photograph was taken with an actual roll of film in a camera and not digitally. A young Jace, no older than five, stands in front of a tree holding the same trophy that's on the shelf. He has bright blonde hair and pudgy cheeks that smile so big you can see his missing front tooth. I recognize his clothing as being motocross gear, but it looks nothing like the style of gear today. The colors are bold and tacky, the pants look like they're straight from the eighties. I squint my eyes and try to make out the surroundings in the grainy photograph. I can barely see an old score tower near a row of trees. Mountains fill up the distance and I know he's not in Texas.

"Fifth place," I say, reading the brass on the tiny trophy.

"He was so proud to get that trophy," Julie says. "It was his prized possession. It's funny to think that just two years later, the boy would have died if he got fifth place. He was always winning or coming in second."

"Yeah I can't imagine Jace getting fifth place now," I say. "He'd probably be mad for days."

"That's because it'll never happen," Jace says, throwing me a confident smile.

"Maybe not after you've raced a million times. Just getting a trophy out of fifteen other kids on your first ever race was pretty impressive," Julie says. She seems ten years younger when she's bragging about her son. And Jace seems ten years younger with how shy he gets when she talks about him like this. It shows a vulnerability to the man I consider my rock, the man who always knows what to do and always has my back. I love seeing this side of him.

I take a step backward and lean my head back against Jace's chest. Julie's phone rings and she excuses herself to answer it.

"Let me show you my favorite place," Jace says, sliding his hand down my back and guiding me back toward the big part of the kitchen.

"And where might that be?" I ask. He nods toward the metal staircase that spirals sharply up a pole and disappears into the ceiling above. "Is this the place you bring all the girls?" I ask, trying to play it off like I don't care, but I do. I really do.

"Does my mom count?" he asks.

I shake my head and climb up the stairs quickly, more eager to see what awaits at the top now that I know it won't' be Jace's secret make out spot. The stairs lead to a tiny room that overlooks balcony on the second floor. We push open the sliding glass doors and step out onto a covered porch. There's a hammock to the right and a plush outdoor couch to the left. The view is amazing. It faces the back of the neighborhood, which unlike the front, it doesn't face another row of houses. All I can see for miles is the beauty of Sacramento.

Jace plops down into the hammock and steadies himself, resting his hands behind his head. I lean my hands on the balcony railing and look out at the world beyond, taking it all of the beauty the landscape has to offer.

"Mind if I join you?" I ask Jace a few moments later.

"I don't know," he says, squishing his lips to the right. "I really loved the view from here."

"You can see over the railing from the hammock?" I ask.

He shakes his head and that sneaky grin of his appears on his gorgeous face. "No, but I had a sexy view of that ass."

Heat fills my cheeks. "Yeah, well this *ass* would like to cuddle with you."

"Come on over," he says, doing his best to slide over in the hammock. "As long as I get to grab it, I'll be alright."

I slide into the hammock and curl up on my side, allowing Jace, my ever horny fiancé, to grab my butt and slide his hand into my back pocket. When his bicep is relaxed it makes for a great pillow. Soon, watching the view from the slats in the balcony railing grows tiresome and I focus on the gentle swaying of the hammock in the breeze. My eyelids feel heavy and the last thing I remember thinking is how the weather in Sacramento is just perfect for a nap outdoors.

"BABE."

My eyes flutter open briefly before closing again. The sound comes again, a deep rumble of a familiar voice. "Babe. Wake up."

The words register in my brain and even though I don't really want to wake up from this glorious nap, I know I need to. Jace hovers over me, his dirty blonde hair glimmering in the glow of the setting sun. "Hey there," he says, smirking. "I can't believe you fell asleep."

"Sorry," I mumble. We're still in the hammock, so even when I try to roll over in an effort to sit up, my body just twists like an overturned turtle and I'm back where I started, pressed against Jace's chest. "How late is it?"

"It's six-thirty. I just heard my dad's truck pull into the driveway, so I figured we should get up. I don't want a lecture about how napping isn't healthy for someone my age."

This makes me try a little harder at getting out of the hammock, and this time I'm met with much less resistance. I swing my feet over the edge and stand up, offering a hand to Jace so he can follow my lead. "I definitely don't want my first time meeting your dad to be when I'm lying asleep with you. That's just...awkward."

Jace laughs. "Yeah, I didn't think about that." He pats his hair down and smooths out his shirt. "How do I look?"

"Cute," I say.

He gives me a sleepy smile and runs a hand through his hair. "Guess I'll take that."

Jace's dad is practically an older clone of Jace. Which is weird, because it feels like I'm seeing into the future and getting a glimpse of what Jace will look like when we're in our late forties. Just like Julie had insisted on being called her first name, Jace's dad takes the same approach.

"Call me Gary," he says when Jace introduces us. His

smile reaching his eyes. "Mr. Adams makes me sound like an old man."

"You are an old man," Jace says. Gary is an inch or two taller than Jace is, and this is the first time that I can recall seeing Jace have to look up to someone. His dad slugs him in the shoulder for his old man joke, and then he looks back at me. "Jace told us you were pretty, but he didn't say how pretty."

I know he's just saying it because that's something dads say to their son's girlfriends, but it makes me smile like an idiot regardless. "Thanks," I mutter, taking a step closer to Jace. For a moment, I feel like a little kid who wants to dart behind her mom and cling onto her leg to hide from the grown up who is talking to me. But my mom isn't here in Sacramento with me. I'm an adult now and I have to face my fears head on.

"So what's for dinner?" Gary asks, silencing his cell phone for the third time in as many minutes. "I'm starving."

"Italian?" Julie asks.

"Oh my God, yes," Jace says, practically salivating over one single word. "Is that cool with you?" he asks me. I nod. "I could eat anything."

"Italian, it is!" Gary says. "I'm turning off this damn phone now. Stupid things aren't worth the effort."

"Who keeps calling you?" I ask.

"Work junk." He waves his hand as if the callers aren't important enough to name. "But I don't have time for that tonight. Tonight is all about spending time with my new family member."

We all climb into the Escalade again, only this time Jace's dad takes the passenger seat and I get to share the backseat with Jace. I'm really starting to wonder why I had been so nervous to meet these people in the first place. Jace is the most loving, understanding person I've ever known. It only makes sense that his parents, the people who raised him to be the man he is today, would share the same personality traits. After days of anxious worrying about meeting his parents, I finally feel like I can relax.

That is of course, until we get to the restaurant.

CHAPTER 15

I don't even realize it at first. After parking in the back of a crowded parking lot at what Julie assures me is one of the best Italian restaurants in the state, I hang back to allow her to tell me about her favorite dishes while Jace and his dad walk up ahead of us. I don't really pay attention to the thin, well-dressed girl walking in close proximity to my fiancé. After all, this is a busy restaurant and people all around us are heading toward the hostess stand outside, or walking back to their car after eating dinner. A girl walking next to Jace is not a big deal.

But then, while Julie is gushing about the chicken parm, I notice the wave of silky honey-colored hair swoosh to the right. The girl smiles and gets a little bounce in her step as she walks. Then she touches Jace's arm.

She. Touches. My. Fiancé.

Julie's voice fades into background static as I stare at the girl just a couple yards ahead of me. Tunnel vision takes over and all I can focus on is her perfect hair and her perfect calves protruding out from the shortest damn shorts ever. She's talking and laughing and acting as if she and

Jace are the best of friends. Who the hell does this girl think she is?

And why the hell hasn't Jace turned around and–oh. Okay, then.

Just as I was thinking it, Jace's steps slow and he turns around, extending his right arm toward me, waiting for me to catch up. The girl slowed down as well, but she took one look at me, and then another, and then looked back at Jace.

"It was cool meeting you," she tells him, before tucking a strand of hair behind her ear and parting off toward the outside seating area. Jace's parents walk around us and head toward the hostess stand to reserve a table for us. I feel bad about having ignored Julie for the last few minutes, and I hope she hadn't said anything that would have made it obvious that I wasn't paying attention.

"Old girlfriend?" I say. I smile like I'm joking but I know we both know I'm completely serious. What can I say? I'm a jealous paranoid freak and Jace already knows this so he should know what he's getting into by now.

He shakes his head. "Just a fan."

"A fan, eh?" I lift an eyebrow. "A fan of...being your ex-girlfriend?"

He laughs. "You don't have anything to worry about babe. She asked if I was Jace Adams and I said yeah and that was about it."

I narrow my eyebrows. "I don't think I like California girls."

He grabs my hand, locking his fingers between mine. "Neither do I."

Dinner gets a little awkward just after the food arrives. Jace's dad has had a glass and a half of wine and it makes him more talkative than all the rest of us put together. "So are you guys going to stay in that cowboy state forever?"

"You know what's weird?" Jace says in response to the question. "I haven't seen a single cowboy in Texas. It's seriously disappointing." He doesn't even seem affected by the way his dad talked about my home state, but I'm a little offended about it. I mean, sure we have a reputation for being cowboys, but that's really not what the state is like anymore. We're regular people. And besides, what exactly does he mean in asking if we're staying there forever?

"No cowboys, eh?" Gary takes a sip from his wine. "Sure seemed like it when I was there."

"Just because Grandfather was a cowboy doesn't mean everyone else is," Jace says. "Look at Bayleigh. She's as city girl as they come. Took me forever to get her to stop fretting over her hair and makeup at the track."

"Are your parents cowboys?" Gary asks me.

I shake my head. "No, sir."

"Good." He nods more to himself than to us. "Now that we've established how no one here is a cowboy, you need to sell that shack in Texas and move back here where you belong."

It takes me a minute to realize what he means. Our apartment isn't a shack, not that he's even seen it, and besides, we don't own it so we can't sell it.

"I was thinking of renting it out," Jace says without missing a beat. Only then do I understand the full meaning of Gary's suggestion. The beautiful two story home in Salt Gap, Texas is not anything close to being a shack. But it was Jace's grandfather's house before he died and left it to Jace and I know that Gary didn't get along with his father. So I guess in his eyes, the gorgeous home is just a shack.

"We don't live there," I say. "We have an apartment in Mixon."

"I know, but I'm talking about Jace's inheritance. You need to get rid of it, Son. It's just wasting your time right now."

"I think renting it out is a nice idea," Julie interjects, placing a hand on her husband's arm. "It'll be a nice source of secondary income."

Gary shakes his head. "I'd be happier if the damn place was gone for good."

"Unfortunately for you, honey, this is not your decision." I don't have to be related to her to know that she's giving him a look that says *shut up right now.*

Jace lets out an exasperated sigh. Something tells me this isn't the first time he's had a conversation like this with his dad. I don't know what happened to end Gary's relationship with Jace's grandfather, but it's a little sad that the man can't just get over it already.

The awkwardness has reached epic proportions. It would be easy to excuse myself and say I need to use the restroom. I could take my time walking there and back and hopefully when I returned, the conversation would have changed.

"Excuse me for a minute," I begin, sliding my chair out from the table. "I need to use the restroom." I go to stand up, but the waitress rushes up and blocks my exit. Only when I look up, I realize she's not a waitress at all. She's just some girl.

"I'm so sorry to interrupt your dinner," she says, staring straight at Jace as she speaks.

"No worries at all, Ashley," Gary says with a massive smile on his face that wasn't there a few moments earlier. "It's good to see you, girl."

"Thanks, Mr. Adams," the girl gushes. "Hey, Jace."

The way she says his name makes my heart stop. Immediately, a stab of painful awareness pierces into me. This is not some type of girl who stops Jace in a parking lot and tells him she loves watching him race. She's not going to smile and blush and ask him for an autograph or a picture to post on her Facebook. This girl knows him. She used to, at least.

She places her hand on the back of his chair when he turns around to greet her. He looks a little surprised to see her, but surprise isn't the worst expression he could have. For all I know, she could be his cousin or something. He gives her a tight-lipped smile. "Hey, Ashley."

Definitely not a cousin.

She puts her hands on her hips like she's about to gripe at him for something stupid like drinking from the milk carton. "So are you finally back here for good?"

Jace snorts a little laugh. "Nah, not right now."

"Why *not?*" She's whining like a twelve-year-old girl. I roll my eyes and lean back in my chair. No one notices my own prominent display of acting like a child, probably because everyone's eyes are on this chick. She's dressed like a teenager, in tight jeans with rhinestones all over the pockets and a skimpy tank top that shows so much cleavage, you can tell there's totally a push up bra under there. But the fine lines around her eyes and the creases around her lips when she smiles makes her look older. I can't really pin her age, but the way she's smiling at Jace would make me hate her even if she were old enough to be his grandmother.

I'm startled out of my silent fuming over this girl when Julie taps my arm. "Honey, weren't you going to the restroom?"

I shake my head. Funny how the urge to pee can completely disappear and be replaced with an animalistic urge to rip another woman's head off. "I think I'll stay and meet Jace's new friend."

I say it a little louder than necessary, hoping it reaches my fiancé and gives him the hint to introduce me. But I don't think he even hears me. Julie's eyebrows crinkle together. "Ashley's not a new friend. They've known each other for years."

"Good to know," I say. Jace still hasn't introduced me. You want to know why? Because he's wrapped up in a conversation with this Ashley girl and he hasn't even bothered to look in my direction since she showed up. Did he forget about me?

"Jace." I don't really mean to say it out loud, but maybe I do. When he turns toward me, eyebrows lifted, I realize I don't have a single thing to say. At least not anything I could say in front of other people. "Um, where's the restroom?" It's a dumb question, but it's the first thing that comes to mind. He motions toward the front of the restaurant. "I think it's near the door."

Ashley jiggles her hand which is still on the back of his chair. The dozen golden bangles around her wrist dance around, clanking together in what I can only assume is the tune to the national anthem of skanks. "Oh, Jacey!" Ashley touches her arm, bouncing on her heels. "I can't believe I forgot to tell you about Kristen!"

And just like that, Jace's attention is back on this girl who everyone seems to know but no one is introducing to me. I grab my fork and press it into the tablecloth, trying like hell not to listen to the stupid crap Ashley is rambling on about. She says something about a girl named Kristen who got into some fancy dance academy and then I don't hear the rest because I take out my phone and text Becca.

Me: So we're getting dinner and some girl comes up

and is talking to Jace and his whole family. She knows them apparently.

Becca: It's probably a family friend? Prob not a big deal, Bay

Me: Is tall, gorgeous and blonde not a big deal?

Becca: You're gorgeous and blonde!

Me: I'm dirty-blonde.

Becca: Who cares? Jace is with you. So stop worrying. Stress isn't good for you.

I know she's right and I know she's trying to help. But it doesn't really help. I just want someone to side with me and tell me I'm not crazy for hating this girl who is interrupting our dinner. If I had any guts, I'd just introduce myself to her, let her know I'm Jace's fiancé. And if I was really bold, I'd ask her to leave.

Ashley's voice filters back in my mind and I glance up and find that she's still talking like some kind of unstoppable children's talking Elmo. "So you guys should totally come by and see my art, okay? I won't take no for an answer."

Her art? I look around at the faces of Jace's family and they're all nodding and smiling and saying what a great idea it is. "What are ya'll talking about?" I ask, looking exclusively at Jace and not at the skank hovering around behind his chair.

"Ashley invited us to her photography exhibit."

"Oh, that's too bad because we're leaving tomorrow." I give him a tight-lipped smile.

He nods. "Yeah but our flight isn't until five, so we have some time."

I never take my eyes off of him. I know everyone is staring at me but I don't care. "We can't make it."

"Sure you can," Gary says, holding up his wine glass when the server passes by. "We'll stop by on our way to the airport."

"Jacey, that would be awesome!" Ashley squeals. "You have to see those shots of you I took–you look amazing. I'll make you a CD tonight so you can have them, okay? Just make sure you give the credit to me."

"Jesus Christ," I mutter under my breath. There are a million questions I will ask Jace once we are back home in privacy, things such as *who the hell is this girl and why did she take photos of you?* But right now, I am so livid I will surely explode if I don't get the hell out of here. My chair slides backward and I stand up sharply. "I have to pee," I announce just before I walk away. Luckily the anger boiling inside of me keeps any hint of tears far far away. I am nowhere close to crying. I'm more likely to punch a random stranger in the face.

Once I'm inside the bathroom, I take out my phone and open it to Becca's text. Now I know what to say that will put her back on my side, however irrational my side may be.

Me: She keeps calling him Jacey.
Becca: I. Hate. Her.

CHAPTER 16

Our brief visit with Jace's parents flies by much sooner than I had anticipated. Now that it's the morning of our last day here, I'm not so sure Sacramento is all it's cracked up to be. I stand on the second floor balcony, sipping on some hot chocolate and watching the sunrise in the distance. Sure, the scenery is beautiful but the people are beautiful, too. And they all seem to have a thing for my boyfriend. Well, at least the ones that I've met. As I look around the massive house and take in the scenery, all I feel is a deep longing for home.

I don't feel safe here. I feel exposed and ignored at the same time. Jace had spent most of last night cuddling up to me and making not-so-subtle attempts to get me naked. But the last thing I wanted to do was have sex with someone who had spent a good deal of the night before chatting with some blonde chick he never bothered introducing to me.

I take in a deep breath and sigh. I'm still pissed about that. The whole time that Ashley chick was talking to us, he never once decided to bring me into the conversation.

That is so unlike him. I probably should have swallowed my pride and brought it up last night, had him explain it all to me and tell me that she was no one to worry about. But I let my anger and annoyance rule and instead, I fell asleep early to avoid talking to Jace.

And now I'm awake at the crack of dawn. It wouldn't have been fun to lie in bed next to the man who ignored me while talking to that Ashley girl. I try to tell myself that it was all some misunderstanding, because every single time I get upset about something like this, it always ends up being a misunderstanding. But my brain refuses to believe things like that.

When my hot chocolate is gone, I slip back inside and rinse out my cup in the kitchen. I make sure the bag from my hot chocolate mix is in the trash and that the place looks as immaculate as it was when I first walked in this morning. As far as I know, everyone in the house is still asleep.

With nothing else to do, I walk up the stairs and slip back out on the balcony. Not even a minute later, the sliding glass door creaks open, startling me so much I jump. I turn around expecting Jace.

"Oh!" I say when it is most definitely not Jace standing on the balcony with me. "I'm sorry, I hope I didn't wake you."

"Nope, you're fine," Julie says, pulling a metal chair away from the wall and sliding it to where I'm standing. She holds a coffee mug steady while she wipes the morning dew from the chair and sits down. "I love drinking my coffee out here in the mornings."

"It's a pretty view," I say. I wonder how long I have to stay around out here before I can politely excuse myself and go back to the room I'm sharing with Jace. Not that there's anything wrong with Julie, but I am so not in the mood to talk to anyone right now.

"Are you feeling well?" Julie asks, glancing from my eyes to my stomach.

I nod. "I don't really get morning sickness. Usually I get sick in the afternoons."

"Oh, well that's no good for your flight," she says, furrowing her brows. "You should see if they'll let you change your flight date. Maybe something for early tomorrow morning."

I shake my head so furiously I fear it might fall off. "No, that's fine. I'll be fine."

"Don't want to stick around?" she asks. Her eyes give me a coy look over the rim of her coffee mug. "Are you missing home?"

"More than you know," I say quietly.

"Aww, is it really that bad? You guys don't have the puppy yet, do you?"

"No. Wait, what? Why would we have a puppy?"

She makes the motion of zipping her lips closed. "No reason. I just thought maybe ya'll had a pet or something to get back home to. Kennels are expensive around here. I don't know about down there in Texas…"

"Did Jace tell you I want a puppy?" We had talked about it a few weeks ago when Jace's schedule had picked up a lot in preparation for the national motocross races. I was home by myself a lot and wanted to get a puppy or a kitten for companionship while he was away. He kind of shot down that idea instantly. He said a pet would be fun for a short while but then taking care of it and a baby would drive me insane. I had agreed and told him that he was right; a baby and a puppy that would need training and daily walks would be a difficult responsibility to handle. But I still wanted one. I'm always thinking about bringing it up again and sometimes I drop hints by leaving my computer screen open to the local pet shelter's adoption page, or making a big deal when I see photos of cute puppies online. Jace is a rock though. When he's made up his mind, he won't budge.

"He might have mentioned something about you wanting one," she says. "I was just trying to think of reasons why you're ready to go home so quickly. We love having you here, you know." She leans forward in her chair and lowers her voice. "And forget all of Gary's bullshit about selling that house in Salt Gap. If Jace wants to keep it, then let him. He doesn't need to do something he doesn't want to do just because his father wants him to."

"Good to know," I say. "Jace doesn't really talk about that house much. But I wouldn't want him to sell it. It's where we met."

Even though I am still mad at him, my heart melts a bit when I remember the day I met him. It wasn't exactly love at first sight, but I did think he was crazy hot, walking around shirtless and sweaty from riding his dirt bike in the backyard. He was a guy who had his shit together—at least that's what it had seemed like. Turns out he had just as many holes in his life as I had in mine. Together we make a whole person. And soon we'll have another person to share our lives with.

"My god, you are adorable," Julie says, pressing her hand to her heart.

"What do you mean?"

"The look on your face right now was…" She shakes her head slightly while taking another sip of her coffee. "You really love my son. There's no denying that."

"I didn't know anyone was denying it," I say with a shy smile.

"No, of course not. I am so happy for you, dear."

"Thank you," I say, feeling a mixture of happiness and awkwardness at our intimate conversation.

"It's too bad you can't stay longer," she says. "There are so many places in California that I'd love to show you."

"Maybe we can come back another time," I say.

"You better come back! I hope to see my grandbaby as much as possible. I'd even love it if you and the baby came over and spent weeks with me while Jace was working his butt off in Texas."

I smile at the sentiment. I know she's just exaggerating, but it's a cool thing to hear. "Can I ask you something?" I swallow and then quickly add, "About Jace?"

She tries to sip from her coffee mug, but there's no more left. "Of course. What's up?"

I kind of want to shrink back and tell her never mind. Avoiding the pressing question in my head might work for a little bit, but eventually it would come right back to haunt me until I found out the answer. "That Ashley girl...who is she? Did they used to date or something?"

Julie's eyes seem to widen in surprise and then relax a bit as she takes in my questions. "I thought you were acting weird at dinner last night. Did you ask Jace about her?"

I shake my head and look toward the wooden floor beneath my toes. "No, but he didn't even introduce me to her. That was the worst part. Usually he introduces me to everyone. Usually he seems proud about it."

"Ashley is a...unique person," Julie begins. She sets her coffee mug on the balcony railing and I wonder if she's taking her time talking because she's trying to lessen the blow of telling me that Ashley was his former soul mate or something. "She never really knew how to pick up on signs and well, Jace isn't good at saying no, I guess."

If I didn't have morning sickness before, I do now.

"What exactly does that mean? They dated because Jace couldn't say no?"

She shakes her head. "No, dear. They never dated. But we've known her since she and Jace were little kids out at the motocross track. Her dad runs the races so we were always over there visiting and the kids played in the sand when they were little. She always wanted to play with Jace and he was always so annoyed with her."

This makes me smile, but tales of little kids hardly equates to how they are around each other today. "Jace doesn't seem like someone who would be friends with a person he didn't like," I say. I hope the tone in my voice doesn't make me sound like I'm being disrespectful, but her backstory so far isn't helping calm my fears.

"No, he normally isn't that kind of a person," Julie says with a nod. "But I think he felt sorry for her. Ashley was always a super eager little kid and then when they were about thirteen, she obviously had a big crush on him and she followed him around the track like crazy. At one point she started telling everyone she was his girlfriend. Oh man, you should have seen how angry he got. I remember him stomping back to our truck at the races, his face all red and his jaw clenched tightly. I asked him what was wrong and he said that all the boys he raced with were making fun of him for being Ashley's boyfriend. Apparently that was the first time he had heard that she declared them boyfriend and girlfriend."

As she's telling me the story, it dawns on me that Jace must have a pretty close relationship with his mom. I would never have told my mom those kinds of things when I was kid. I don't really tell her much about my life now. It's not that I don't want her to know it's just...weird.

Julie's eyes roam over the horizon as she talks. "You should have seen how mad he was. Ashley and her dad had already left for the day but he spent the entire week waiting until the next race so he could yell at her for lying about being his girlfriend. He wanted to embarrass her in front of her friends the same way his friends had embarrassed him." She sighs and her face softens into something like regret. "Of course then when the weekend came, Ashley wasn't there. We found out that she'd had a tumor on her lung. It was cancer. She had to have surgery and chemo and when she finally did come back to the track, she didn't have any hair. He wasn't about to yell at her then."

"Well whatever happened with the rumors she started?" I asked.

Julie shrugged. "I think he told her privately something about how she can't tell people they were dating when they weren't. Then of course, she begged him to be her boyfriend and he told her was he too busy for girls." Julie snorted in laughter. "That was his excuse for a long, long time. He was going to be a professional racer. He didn't have time for girls. Of course he would have had time if he didn't spend every waking moment of his life on a dirt bike. For a while there I thought I'd never get grandkids." Her lips purse into a smile and she reaches forward and squeezes my shoulder. "Luckily my fears have been resolved now."

I can't believe I'm about to say this, but well, we're already talking and no one else is around so it's kind of the perfect moment to speak my heart. "Are you really not mad about this?" I gesture to my stomach which looks much smaller under folds of fabric from Jace's t-shirt that I stole to use as pajamas. "I mean...we're young and we're not married yet and..."

"Bayleigh, you listen to me." Julie's eyes flicker with an expression I can't quite place. It's a little scary, but not in the traditional sense. "Gary and I raised Jace to be the man he is today and I trust him quite a bit. I would trust him with my life. He makes good decisions and I've only known you a few days but I can tell he made a good decision with you. So no, I'm not mad about your pregnancy. Why on earth would I be mad about gaining a precious grandson?"

I don't even realize I'm crying until I blink and tears fall down my cheeks. Then, as if that tiny teardrop managed to rip open all of the emotions I'd been holding back, I burst into tears. Julie's out of her chair in an instant, her warm arms encircling me in the most mothering way possible. "Oh, honey," I hear her murmur into my hair. "Everything will be just fine, I promise."

"I don't even know why I'm crying," I sputter, pulling away from her hug. I shake my head and try unsuccessfully to wipe away my tears with the back of my hand. "I'm just…"

"I get it." Julie smiles, tilting her head. "Pregnancy sucks. But you look at it this way…you'll be a young mother, which is awesome. I know because I am one." She puts her hand on her hip and winks. "When all your friends are wiping snotty noses and changing diapers, you'll have a kid who can take care of themselves. It's amazing." Her eyes light up a few moments later. "Unless of course, ya'll decide to have more kids which would make me, Grandma, very excited."

"I can't even imagine that right now," I say with a laugh. "One epic life changing thought at a time, please."

Julie laughs. "I have no advice for you on that one. Jace was our only child so I have no experience in raising more kids. But he was so easy. Such an easy baby. Hopefully yours will be, too."

I nod even though I'm not really sure what part of raising a baby could ever be easy. I'm not even sure I still know how to change a diaper. It's been a long time since my little brother wore them. I'd like to think I did a good job in raising him as a baby, but truthfully, any time something was hard, I'd make Mom do it.

"So are you excited about the wedding?" Julie asks.

I nod. "I'm really excited about my dress and everything, but it's kind of scary because it doesn't feel like it's as big of a deal as it should be. I keep seeing wedding shows on television and it's all so big and fancy and important...my wedding planning hasn't been like that at all."

"That's because television makes everything out to be more dramatic than it really is." She waves a hand through the air dismissively. "Your wedding doesn't have to be that. Besides, a small wedding like yours will be amazing and you'll make so many great memories of it."

"So it'll be small?" I ask casually, gnawing on my bottom lip. "Can you tell me anything else about it?"

"Oh my God, I forgot!" Julie's eyes widen and she slaps a hand over her mouth. "You don't know the venue! I can't believe I almost said it out loud. Jace would have *killed* me!"

"So everyone already knows my wedding location but me?" I laugh. "This is probably the weirdest way to plan a wedding."

"Don't worry, you'll love it," Julie assures me. "But let's not tell Jace that I almost said too much."

The glass door slides open and we both spin around, eyes wide and guilty expressions that could be seen a mile away.

Jace stands at the doorway, a cup of coffee in one hand. He lifts an eyebrow. "Am I interrupting something?"

"Nope," Julie says, glancing at me with a smile. "Just talking about...a sale at Nordstrom."

"Bayleigh doesn't shop at Nordstrom," Jace says skeptically.

Julie shrugs. "All the more reason to talk about it."

He rolls his eyes, showing us that he doesn't believe a single word of our shenanigans. When he wraps his arm around my waist and kisses me good morning, the smell of his coffee makes my stomach hurt. But I smile anyway so it won't upset him.

"Well, whatever you were talking about, I'm glad the two of you are having fun."

"Oh we definitely are," Julie says, smiling.

"Yeah and by the way," I tell Jace. My heart starts pounding in my chest but I don't care. I'm going to say this. "I'm not going to Ashley's stupid photography show."

"Yeah," Julie says defiantly. "Forget her."

CHAPTER 17

One *week before the wedding*

I CAN ALWAYS TELL WHEN IT'S SATURDAY MORNING compared to every other morning. These are the days when Jace doesn't have to wake up before the sun, throw on some clothes and rush off to work. These are his off days. Well, usually. Spending Saturday mornings in bed with him is one of my favorite things. The bed is always warmer when he's in it, snuggled up next to me. I can't imagine a better paradise than being curled against his chest in our plush mattress, in the place we've made a home.

Unfortunately, today is the last Saturday Jace and I will have as single people. Next Saturday we'll be married. The unfortunate part is not because of the marriage, obviously. It's because this is a freaking Saturday, unofficially known as my snuggle day, and Jace is still up at the butt-crack of dawn. His best man and best friend Park is arriving today and Jace has to pick him up from the airport because unfortunately for us, he's also not of legal age to rent a car.

He leans over my side of the bed and kisses me on the forehead. "Be back before you know it," he whispers.

"Not true," I whisper back. "I already miss you so you can't be back before I know it. Because I know it right now."

"What am I gonna do with you?" he says, assaulting me in an onslaught of kisses to my cheek, neck, shoulder and lips.

I giggle profusely, twisting left and right because he hasn't shaved in a couple of days and his scraggly facial hair tickles like crazy. When he stops, I catch my breath and push him away. "Go get your friend," I say, rolling my eyes. "Ya'll better bring me back a cheeseburger."

"It's six in the morning," Jace says. "What do you want a cheeseburger for?"

I sit up on my elbows and give him the most serious look I can muster. "Are you seriously going to question your pregnant fiancé's food cravings?" I stick out my tongue.

"You are the biggest dork in the world, but I love you so much."

"I love you, too," I say, rolling back over in bed, pulling the covers up to my neck as sleep starts to fall over me again. "Cheeseburger," I whisper as I snuggle under the covers some more. I'm pretty sure I feel him plant a kiss on my cheek one more time before he slips out the door. I think I smile, but I'm too sleepy to know for sure.

I slip on an oven mitt and pull out the tray of cinnamon rolls a few seconds before the timer goes off. My phone still hasn't rang since this morning when Becca called to let me know she was leaving her house and would be here soon. We have a whole day of last minute wedding prep to do, and she was supposed to arrive like, right now. That's why I timed the cinnamon rolls perfectly.

With the cinnamon rolls on the counter and the oven mitt off my hand, I grab my phone to check it for any missed messages. No word from Becca. I frown and begin frosting our breakfast, hoping she gets here soon. I don't know if it's because I'll be a mother soon, or if I'm just going crazy, but I hate waiting on people. All I can ever think about is that they probably got in some horrific wreck and are lying dead on the road right now, unable to tell me.

There's a knock at my door, and I leap off the barstool, running toward the door at full speed. I swing open the door without checking the peephole first. "Thank God you're not dead!" I say in a voice that's terrifyingly like my mother's.

Becca rolls her eyes and pushes through the door with about six big bags in tow. "Why would I be dead?"

"Because you took so long to get here," I say, helping her with the bags.

"You're ridiculous. Do I smell breakfast?"

"Yep. You'll be happy to know I didn't burn the bottoms this time."

"Woohoo!" She high-fives me. "You're going to be an excellent wife one of these days. Now we just need to teach you the super tricky skill of boiling water."

Now I'm the one rolling my eyes. "I know how to boil water."

She slaps a hand to her chest in surprise. "Jace is such a lucky man!"

I grab a frosted cinnamon roll and shove it in her mouth. "Here, eat this so I don't have to keep listening to you talk."

Becca helps herself to two cups of coffee while I drink hot chocolate in order to avoid caffeine for the baby. I never knew she was such a huge coffee drinker until lately. She claims she picked up the habit at the place where she works. Apparently they all drink coffee like fiends over there. I'm a little jealous of her job because when she talks about it, you can tell she really loves it. I hope I will love my job just as much when I'm working full time at the motocross track.

"So what all did you bring me?" I ask after we've eaten. I drop to the floor and start digging through the bags. One is a paper shopping bag made of pearly thick paper with satin ribbon handles.

"Oooh!" Becca swoons, darting to the floor next to me. "Those are the RSVPs! Every single person we invited has replied. That has to be some kind of world record or something."

I dig into the bag and pull out about fifty envelopes, all addressed to Jace and me in Becca's lovely cursive handwriting. The RSVP cards are printed on the same cardstock and in the same elegant style as the invitations, but I never got to see them because the invitations had the address of the venue. The paper is hand dyed with turquoise at the top and purple on the bottom, the colors fading between the two in a beautiful ombre.

One part of me absolutely loves that Jace planned the location of our wedding in secret and the other part of me is going completely crazy, dying to know where it'll be. It is supposed to be a small wedding with a small venue, that's all I know. We both didn't want some crazy big location, but when I search online for small wedding places in

Texas, nothing quite looks like something Jace would choose.

We open all of the RSVPs and take note of who is coming and who "regretfully declined" by checking that box on the paper. Some of Jace's older relatives who aren't healthy enough to make the trip declined as we already knew they would. When I open the RSVP from Becca's mom, I start laughing.

The checkbox for Regretfully Decline was checked and then scratched out and the box for Joyfully Accepts was checked. In small lettering at the bottom of the paper, Becca's mom had written: *SHIT I'm sorry, I checked the wrong box on mistake. Of course I am coming! Love you!*

"Your mom is so scatterbrained," I say, placing her RSVP to the side. It is definitely going into the wedding memories scrapbook that I swear I'll get around to making one of these days.

"Tell me about it," Becca says. "She bought you a wedding card the other day and was totally confused when I told her she already bought a card for you like two months ago. Now she'll probably give you both of them since she can't choose which one is her favorite."

My phone rings and since Becca is closer to the coffee table, she hands it to me, sing-songing the words, "It's your lover-boy."

I'm laughing at how stupid she is when I answer the phone.

"Hey," Jace says. He sighs. "I'm at the airport and I'm confused as shit."

"What does that mean?"

"I've been waiting for his flight, number 4572, and it just landed but I can't find Park. I watched everyone who came out of the plane and then I've been standing by the baggage claim and he's not here."

"Did you try calling him?" I ask.

"Like a million times. His phone goes straight to voicemail."

"Are you sure you have the right flight?" I know my questions are pointless because I'm sure Jace has already thought of them, but I ask anyway.

"Yeah," he says, his voice dejected. "He had emailed me his flight information. This is definitely the right place he should have landed. I even asked some of the other passengers who walked by. I don't know where he is, but I'm thinking he never got on this plane."

"Wow…" I gnaw on my bottom lip and Becca gives me a curious look. "What are you going to do?"

"I guess I'll stay around a little longer. Maybe I missed him somehow. I'll keep trying his phone. Part of the reason I called you was to make sure my phone is still working because I was starting to think maybe the problem was on my end."

"Good luck, babe." I try to think of something comforting to say. Jace isn't like me. He's not going to jump to the conclusion that Park is dead, lying in a ditch somewhere outside of the airport in California. "I'm sure he'll show up."

"Thanks. I'll call you later and let you know what's up. I love you."

"I love you more," I say, smiling in an attempt to make him feel better.

"You wish!" he says right before he hangs up.

Becca frowns when I tell her what just happened. "I know he's Jace's best friend and all, but what kind of friend just doesn't show up when they're supposed to?"

"Maybe he missed his flight?" I say with a shrug.

"I don't know who this dude is, but he better get here

in time for the wedding or I'll have to kick his ass for ruining my best friend's big day."

"You look scary when you're making threats," I say. "Remind me not to be late to my own wedding."

"You better not be late. I'd hate to have to kick your ass on your wedding day." She pulls out a folded piece of poster board and flattens it on the floor. Five circles with ten squares around each circle have been drawn on what I now recognize as a handmade seating chart. "Now that we have the RSVPs, we can seat your guests."

"I've always thought this was kind of weird," I say, looking over the hand drawn layout and trying to picture what the venue would look like. "Can't we just let people sit where they want to?"

"Apparently not," she says, pointing at the wedding planning binder I had left on the coffee table. "It seems stupid to me too, but we have to do it."

After the pointless endeavor of placing people in chairs based on how well they know and/or like each other, we sit back and admire our seating chart. There's a head table at the front of the other tables and that's where we'll sit. It's small, with only room for me and Jace in the middle and then Park and Becca on either side of us. I like having a short wedding party. We haven't decided where to put my brother. I think he'd like sitting at the head table with us, but I also think he'd rather sit next to Mom and David. I make a note of it so I can call and ask him later. But for now, we've knocked out one more task in the great list of things to do for a wedding.

Jace gets home around lunchtime. To our disappointment, he arrives alone. His phone is clutched in his hand and I've no doubt that he's been trying to reach Park for the whole drive back.

"I wonder what happened to him?" I ask, barely getting the words out before Jace plants a kiss on my lips.

"Something must have happened. Maybe his truck broke down on the way to the airport. And I guess his phone broke at the same time. He wouldn't just ditch...something happened." He moves past me toward the kitchen and grabs a slice of leftover pizza from the fridge. I cringe when he bites into it cold. I so can't eat cold pizza, but Jace loves it. "What are you girls up to?"

"How are you being so casual about this? Aren't you afraid your friend is dead?"

He gives me a look like I'm crazy. "He's not dead. Something obviously came up, but it wasn't death."

"How do you know that?" I ask, hands on my hips.

He takes a huge bite of pizza. "Because I have faith that things will work out just fine. They always do."

As much as I want to argue his logic by bringing up every possible bad thing that could have happened to prevent Park from catching his flight, I decide to keep my mouth shut. If we still haven't heard from Park in twenty four hours then I'll allow myself to freak out. After all, Jace knows his parents and would probably be the first person they called if something bad had happened to him. This comforts me a little.

JUST BEFORE THE THREE OF US ARE ABOUT TO LEAVE TO GET dinner, Jace asks me to leave the room. He has this sneaky smile on his face so I know he isn't mad at me, but I frown and question him anyway. "Why do I have to leave?"

"Because the maid of honor and I have some wedding

plans to discuss," he says, not missing a beat. "I'd totally let you stay if you weren't the bride but...alas, you are."

"Fine, fine," I say, pushing myself out of Jace's lap. "Don't take too long. I'm starving."

"Love ya," Becca says, grinning like a goofball.

I make a big show of slumping out of the room and into my bedroom. I think seriously about pressing my ear to the door to eavesdrop on any information I can over-hear, but then Jace is one step ahead of me. He turns up the volume on the television until all I can hear is an incredibly loud episode of The Simpsons.

While I wait, I slip into the closet and admire my wedding dress. It stays locked up in a black garment bag, but sometimes when Jace isn't around, I take it out and stare at it on the hanger. I'm too scared to touch it or mess with it, so I leave it on the hanger. The last thing I need is to smudge dirt on it, or snag it on a hangnail or rip off sparkles or something.

As I stare at the folds of fabric, I try to imagine myself wearing the gown in exactly six days from now. My hair will be fixed, my makeup will be flawless. I stare down at my raggedy nails—I've been neglecting my cuticles like crazy. But soon, they'll also be perfectly manicured. I will be all fixed up and painted and primed into the most beau-tiful version of myself.

Then I'll get to marry Jace.

This is all so freaking surreal.

"Knock, knock," Jace says from somewhere just outside of the closet. "Are you staring at your wedding dress again?"

"Yes! Go away!" I shout, frantically grabbing the garment bag and zipping it closed. "You can't see it!"

I hear him slump against the wall next to the closet

door. "That thing must be really pretty with how often you stare at it."

"It is," I say, emerging from the closet and shutting the door quickly behind me. "It is absolutely stunning. And I don't look at it that much."

"Yeah right," he says with a little *psh*. "You look at that dress more than you look at me."

"That's because it's clean and smells good," I snap back.

"Ouch," he says, grabbing me by the waist. "Why you gotta be so mean?"

"You think I'm mean? I'll show you mean." I grab the neckline of my tank top and pull it down low, squeezing my elbows together at the same time so it makes my cleavage burst out. "I bet you want to touch these," I tease, taking a step backward.

Jace's eyes light up. "Touch them? I want to bury my face into them."

"Oh you do?" I say slowly, leaning forward just a bit, getting my breasts ever-so-close to Jace's now outstretched hands. He nods and wiggles his eyebrows at me. Then I stand up straight and let my shirt rise back into place. "Too bad. We have to go to dinner now."

"Oh my God, you're so mean to me," he groans, his voice raspy with desire.

"Told ya," I say, poking him in the stomach.

DURING DINNER, BECCA AND I ARE A NONSTOP CHATTERBOX of wedding talk. Jace doesn't add much to the conversation. He doesn't talk at all unless he's asking the server for more root beer. I know he's worried about Park, so I don't call him out on being quiet. I just let him have time to himself to think. Besides, Becca and I have enough to talk about to keep us entertained all night.

"Okay, so," Becca says, setting down her fork and splaying out her hand. She points to her thumb as she begins listing things. "Invitations are done and replied to, Cupcake cake is ordered, food is ordered, music is done, we all have our dresses and tuxedos…" She trails off when she reaches her pinky.

I pick up where she left off. "We're getting flowers the day of, from some apparently awesome floral shop that I'm not allowed to know. And decorations have been either stored at our apartment or Mom's house and you guys will have it set up beforehand since I *still can't see the venue of my own wedding.*" I say that last part sarcastically enough to make Jace look up from his plate. He winks and then goes back to eating.

"Oh I almost forgot," Becca says. "We also have to make that ring box from Pinterest."

"What is Pinterest?" Jace asks.

We both look at him as if he's missing a head or just sprouted a third eye. "You're joking, right? We talk about it all the time."

He shakes his head. "Ya'll talk about everything all the time. There's no way I can keep up."

"Pinterest is that website with all the images in little squares. I'm constantly showing you stuff on it."

"Ahh, okay." Jace nods. "That's a cool website."

"Yeah it is," Becca says. "We've pretty much planned her whole wedding with it."

Jace startles suddenly and slides his chair back from the table. He reaches into his pocket and takes out his phone, squinting when he sees the number calling him. "Nine sixteen. That's a Sacramento area code," he says right before the swipes and answers the call.

Becca's eyes widen and we stare at each other in hopeful anticipation. My stomach crawls up into my throat as I listen to Jace's end of the conversation.

"Hey, man. I'm glad you're not dead."

Relief floods over me, followed by more dread. If Park is alive and well, then why didn't he show up? What if it's because for some reason he doesn't want to be in our wedding?

Jace's features darken. "No shit. What the hell? How many people?"

Becca and I glance at each other. The moments that stretch between Jace's replies seem to take hours instead of seconds. "I'm so sorry, man. Take care of yourself, okay? Seriously, don't worry about us, worry about yourself first and we'll see how you feel in a week."

When he hangs up the call, Becca and I stare at him, but don't dare ask him for information. Luckily, he tells us anyway. "Park was jumped on the way to the airport. A group of three guys. They stole his phone, his wallet, and his truck."

"Holy shit," Becca says. "Is he okay?"

"They bashed him with a baseball bat, he said. But he said he was okay, just bruised. Said one of the guys had a gun so he didn't really fight back." When Jace glances at me, I can tell he's seeking support. Someone to tell him it's going to be okay. And I wonder if this is what married life is like–having each other's back for every situation, and just knowing what the other person wants you to say.

I wrap my arm around his and lean my head on his shoulder. "The good news is that he's okay. It's better that his stuff got stolen than his life, you know? I'm sure he has insurance and stuff for his truck."

"Yeah, he does," Jace says. "He's not worried about all of that. He said he can't get on an airplane without identification and he's not sure how quickly the DMV can get him a new driver's license."

"Oh…" I say as chills creep over my arms. "I'm so sorry, babe."

Jace runs a hand through his hair. "It's okay. I'm just…" He trails off, shaking his head.

"You just want your best friend at your wedding," Becca says for him. "I know I would."

CHAPTER 18

T*hree days before the wedding*

JACE HAS ALWAYS BEEN REALLY GREAT AT KEEPING SECRETS and surprises from me. Like that time he arranged to buy me a car, he had spent weeks figuring out the details and I hadn't noticed a thing. And then when he was having my engagement ring custom designed for me, I hadn't noticed a change in his demeanor. He even claimed he figured out my ring size in my sleep, and I didn't even wake up. He's always been great at keeping a normal face around me, despite having other things going on in his mind.

Until now.

Park was only able to get a temporary paper license from the DMV. They had to order a real driver's license and said it would be two weeks before it was mailed to him. He couldn't find his passport and without a valid photo identification, there's no way he's getting on an airplane.

Jace keeps saying he's okay, but I know he's not. I've never seen him so distraught.

"He could drive here if he had a car," Jace had said earlier this morning. "But he doesn't because some assholes stole it. The cops still haven't recovered it."

"Do you think his parents could rent him a car or something?" I asked. Jace shook his head. "They're out of the country. On a second honeymoon of all things."

"We can always have a party later and invite him. Then we can all hang out." Jace had smiled at my idea and told me he would love that. Then he promptly stood up, announced he was taking a nap and slunk off. Before he went into our bedroom, he called back, "If Park calls my phone, make sure you answer it!"

That was two hours ago. Becca and I are giving ourselves practice manicures for the wedding while Jace naps and I'm trying really hard not to worry about him. Becca's nails are painted a shiny purple with a faint sprinkle of tiny turquoise glitter. I am trying, very unsuccessfully I might add, to paint my nails the same turquoise-purple ombre as my wedding invitations. The technique involves two nail polishes, a sponge, nail polish remover on a Q-tip and a whole lot of cursing.

I think we're both taken aback when Jace's phone, which is on the coffee table, starts ringing. It has been silent ever since Jace left the room. I glance over at the screen and my eyes burst open. "It's Park! Get it!"

"Why do I have to answer it?" Becca says. "I don't even know him."

"I don't know him either," I say, nudging the phone toward her with the back of my hand. "My nails are wet. I can't answer it."

She sighs and picks up the phone. "Um, hello? No...this isn't Bayleigh. It's Becca, the Maid of Honor."

I don't know why butterflies dance around my stomach. It's practically impossible for Park to get here for the wedding. Unless he knows someone who owns a private jet and would happily waste thousands of dollars in jet fuel to get him here, all of our hope is pretty much wasted.

They chat for a few more minutes, but I get so involved in sponging nail polish onto my index finger that I stop paying attention until Becca gasps and says, "Oh my God, I have a great idea! Hold on a second." She holds the phone away from her ear and turns toward me. "Can we keep a secret from Jace?"

"Totally," I say. New waves of excitement roll through me as Becca and I talk with Park on the phone, keeping our voices low in case Jace wakes up. Park just took out a short term lease on a truck so he'd have something to drive until the police found his old truck and the insurance money came through for him to get a new one. It's a seventeen hundred mile trip from Sacramento to Texas, but he's going to spend the next two days driving here. He should arrive the night before the wedding and he'll get a hotel near the venue (which was still kept a secret from me) and then show up in the morning when we're all getting ready.

It's the perfect wedding surprise for my future husband and we're all really excited about it. Now I just have to play it cool like Jace and act as if everything is normal for the next two and a half days. It'll be hard seeing Jace mope around, missing his best friend, but it'll make the surprise all the more worth it if I don't spill the secret before our wedding day.

Becca gives Park her number so he can call her with any questions he has before the wedding. "Drive safely," I tell him before we hang up.

"Trust me," Park says with a laugh. "I will."

CHAPTER 19

One day before the wedding

I CAN'T SLEEP. IT'S FOUR-THIRTY IN THE MORNING AND MY body absolutely refuses to sleep. After a day spent packing and organizing yesterday, I had passed out fairly quickly last night, but now just a few hours later, I am wide awake. Jace breathes deeply, sound asleep next to me in bed. I stare at the ceiling.

I wonder if he's ever spent the night staring at this same ceiling while I slept peacefully next to him. Probably not. Jace doesn't fret or freak out. He's just calm. I draw in a slow breath, hold it a beat and then slowly exhale, trying to channel some of Jace's everyday calm demeanor. It doesn't really help.

I try to ask myself what I'm worrying about exactly, as if there's some kind of specific thing my mind can't quite grasp and that's why I'm wide awake the night before my wedding. It isn't the wedding. It's not the venue mystery or the fact that we're going to be officially married soon. None of that bothers me.

I'm just...bothered.

The room grows quiet and I realize that Jace's deep breathing has stopped. "You awake?" he asks, rolling on his side.

"Sort of," is my reply.

"Are you getting morning sickness in the middle of the night again?"

"No, it's nothing like that. I'm fine."

"Hmm," Jace says, leaning closer to me. I can just see his features in the soft glow of moonlight filtering in through our window. "Not getting cold feet now, are ya?"

"Ha," I say sarcastically. "No way. Are you?"

He shakes his head. I can't really see him but I can hear the sound of his head squishing against the pillow. "Never. But you seem like something is bothering you and you should talk to me."

"Nothing's bothering me..." I mumble, trying to roll over to face the opposite direction, but Jace slips an arm around me and that kind of puts a stop to my plan.

"Talk to me, babe."

I sigh. "It's just that once we're married, all the anticipation over the wedding will be over. Then we'll have to focus on the hard stuff."

"The hard stuff?"

"The baby."

"The baby won't be hard," he says, snuggling up against my shoulder. I snort. "Really? What makes you so confident in that?"

"You are a super beautiful, super smart woman, Bay. I wouldn't trust anyone else to raise my kid."

"What does being beautiful have to do with raising kids?"

He shrugs and kisses my collarbone. "Nothing, I guess. I just felt like saying it."

Maybe it's just the sleep finally catching up with me. Maybe it's just hearing his words and the way that he says them. But my nerves disappear and I feel great enough to finally fall asleep.

My phone bursts to life at seven in the morning. Squinting my eyes shut against the bright sunlight filtering in through the windows, I flop my hand over onto the nightstand, aiming for my phone. When I find it, I mash the screen with my fingers until the alarm shuts off. Only, the sound merely dims. I open my eyes and realize the alarm sound is now coming from the opposite side of the bed. Jace's alarm went off at the same time.

"Wake up, hot stuff," I say, shoving him. He groans and rolls over, trying to ignore me and continue to sleep.

I crawl on top of him, straddling his stomach so I can lean over to his nightstand and turn off his alarm. While I'm at it, I go ahead and slide my hands up his bare chest, leaning forward to nuzzle my face in his neck. "Wake up Mr. Adams," I whisper in his ear.

When his hands slide up my thighs and grab ahold of my butt, I know he's awake even though he hasn't opened his eyes yet. His lips form a sly smile and I bend down to kiss them.

"It's time to go," I say. "We're driving for a quite a while, I've been told."

"Yup," he says, finally opening his eyes. "Are you ready?"

"I just want to brush my teeth real fast, otherwise all my stuff is already in your truck."

"Awesome," he says. He makes a big show about

removing his hands from my ass, whimpering and everything, and then we climb out of bed.

Before I know it, we're on the road. I can't help grinning as I ride shotgun, staring at the man who will soon be my husband.

CHAPTER 20

T*he day of the wedding*

"IT'S A BEAUTIFUL DAY," I SAY, LEANING MY FOREHEAD against the glass and staring up at the sky. "A perfect day for a wedding," I add with a smile. Jace nods. We're just outside of Mixon, pulling onto the interstate. I glance at Jace from the corner of my eyes. "I wonder if the weather will still be good when we get to wherever we're going...I mean, it could be hours and hours away from here for all I know..."

He gives me a look that says he's not buying my excuse to get more information out of him. "Okay, I'll give you this." Jace says. "A tiny hint...of course you might figure it out but I hope not."

"What is it?"

He bites his bottom lip and then says, "We'll be there in about two hours."

I lift an eyebrow. "That doesn't tell me anything. There's like...five million places that are two hours away."

Jace shrugs. "This is my wedding surprise to you. So you'll just have to wait."

I slouch as much as I can in the passenger side of Jace's truck, grabbing a pillow out of the back seat to squish between me and the window. "I'm not good at waiting," I say as I ease myself into the most comfortable position I can manage while sitting up and being buckled in. "So wake me when we get there."

THE BEAUTY OF SLEEPING ON A ROAD TRIP IS VASTLY underrated. Sure, you don't get to experience any of the sights or argue over which gas station looks like you might get murdered if you stop there, or make fun of weird cars you pass by, but so what? Sleeping is bliss. Sleeping is time travel.

I don't feel the truck roll to a stop and I don't wake up when the engine goes silent. I do stir a bit when my passenger door opens. Jace's soft voice nudges me out of sleep. "Wake up, my bride. We're here."

For a brief moment, I've completely forgotten why I'm asleep in the truck. My eyes flutter open and I yawn, a big monster of a yawn that makes my eyes water. Man, I was passed out. Probably because I didn't sleep well last night. Too excited...

Too excited for...

Oh my God! I sit up so quickly my seat belt locks against my neck, halting me with a quick slash of pain across my skin. The wedding is today. How on earth did I forget that very important fact, even if it was only for a few moments?

"You okay, babe?" Jace laughs, brushing the hair out of my eyes. He's standing next to me, tucked inside the open passenger door of his truck while I'm still buckled into my seat. The moment I see him, I feel tears pool in the corners of my eyes. I don't even know why. I'm just happy. And excited.

I wrap my arms around his neck and pull him toward me. When I open my eyes a few moments later, I see a very familiar oak tree.

"Why did we stop here?" I say, pulling back and looking around at the front yard I haven't seen in over a year. "Do we need to pick up something?"

Jace shakes his head. He reaches over and unbuckles my seatbelt, then helps me climb down from the truck. Goosebumps cover every inch of my skin as I look around. My mouth falls open and I'm not sure it'll ever close again.

"What do you think?" Jace says, gesturing to the sight in front of us.

Jace's grandfather's house, the massive manor of a house in Salt Gap, Texas, has been transformed. The shutters are painted, the porch is refinished. Flowerbeds line the perimeter. But that's not even half of what has changed. Clear lights cover every inch of the grand oak trees in the front yard. Purple and turquoise roses overflow glass vases at various places on the wraparound porch and petals the same color line the cobblestone driveway, directing us into the backyard.

A gazebo has been erected in the center of the yard, right where Jace's old dirt bike jumps used to be. Flowers line every walkway. Fifty white chairs with purple and turquoise satin ribbons tied around the backs, all facing toward the gazebo. It's like a scene right out of a fairytale.

Or, you know, a dream wedding magazine.

"Jace." It's all I can manage to say, because my hand covers my mouth in the next instant. It's just all so beautiful, I can't stand it. And to the left, I can see across the yard to my grandparent's house. The place I once considered a prison, had become so much more than I ever could have imagined.

"I know it's not Disney Land," Jace says, wrapping an arm around my waist. "But when I tried to picture where I'd want to marry you, this was my first idea. I thought it would be romantic...to marry you in the same place where I first met you."

I look into his eyes and feel so much love pour through me that I think I might burst. "It's perfect."

Jace's late grandfather's house is no longer the old bachelor's pad that it was the first time I saw it. It's been cleaned out, refinished and remodeled. It smells clean and fragrant inside, no longer a smelly memory of all the cigars that were smoked in it daily. At first I'm blown away by all of the work this would have taken—where was I when Jace was making all of these phone calls and arranging everything?

Jace laughs when I ask him this. "You were usually sitting right next to me," he says. "Watching TV or sleeping or completely ignoring me when I was on the computer."

"You do such boring things on the computer!" I say in protest. "Why would I pay attention to that?"

"Exactly. My friend Matt is a contractor and we communicated through email for the most part. He was in on the secret and knew never to call if you were going to be around."

I draw in a deep breath and shake my head, letting it out again in a sigh. "You never stop amazing me. I mean, how will I ever pay you back for this?"

"Marry me," he says. And he says it like he's serious, too. Not like he's just making a joke. In this very moment, I am one hundred percent sure that Jace Adams, former motocross superstar, truly believes that I can pay him back for all his hard work just by marrying him.

And I am so, so unworthy of a love like this.

CHAPTER 21

The house's bedrooms have been outfitted to be bridal changing rooms. Mine overlooks the front yard and Jace's is upstairs. As I sit on a blush stool getting my hair done by my Aunt Truly, I have a perfect view out of the massive window. I can see my mother, David and Bentley arrive. The caterers come next and they're all dressed in black with purple and turquoise ties.

The band arrives and sets up in the backyard. I can hear them warm up their instruments and vocal cords and Jace was absolutely right. They sound a lot like my favorite band Mumford and Sons.

"Are you nervous?" Aunt Truly asks, bobby pins hanging out of her mouth.

I try not to roll my eyes. "Are you kidding? Of course I am. Not about getting married though."

"Then what for? I was a freaking wreck at my wedding." She pins another curl on top of my head, then grabs the curling iron off the vanity.

"I'm not nervous to marry Jace. I'm nervous about all

the people. The possibility of tripping on my face or doing something else equally embarrassing."

"Aww, that won't happen." Aunt Truly says confidently, as if she's some kind of mind reader or something.

There's a soft knock at the door and I start to turn, but Aunt Truly stops my head with her head. "Nuh-uh," she mumbles as her hands work my hair. "Don't move or I'll mess it up."

Instead, I choose to watch the vanity mirror in front of me to see who's at the door. It's Mom. She's wearing a cerulean dress, heels and her hair is swept into an updo that makes her look ten years younger.

Just like in the movies, Mom bursts into tears at the sight of me. It makes me giggle. This is all so surreal. "Mom, you look really pretty," I say as she rushes up to me, gushing about my hair and my makeup and my dress.

"Ugh, no," she says, still fawning over me. "I am nothing. You, honey are the star of today. You're so beautiful, I can't even…" Yep, it's all over now. She's now a sobbing puddle of motherly tears. "I love you so much," she whispers as she leans in for a light handed hug, darting out of Aunt Truly's way just before the curling iron had a chance to burn her.

"Okay okay," I say, grabbing a tissue and handing it to her. "There will be no crying today!"

Aunt Truly clicks her tongue. "Good luck with that one."

Becca rushes in a few moments later, her face flushed but still beautiful thanks to the amazing makeup job she did on both herself and me. All of those YouTube makeup tutorial videos she spent months watching have really paid off.

"Why are you so frantic?" I ask. I strain to turn to look at her but Aunt Truly puts a stop to that.

Becca looks through the window, and then glances at her phone. "He's not here yet. He should be here. I don't know if I should call him again. Should I call him again? Would that be annoying of me? Maybe he got lost."

"Park?" I ask, even though the clarification isn't necessary. Of course she's talking about Park. She nods. "I hope he gets here soon. I don't want your wedding ruined."

"Park will not make or break my wedding, trust me. It would suck if he doesn't get here on time just because I wouldn't be able to surprise Jace." I wave my hand in front of her face so she'll stop watching the road and look at me. "Seriously, Becca. No stressing! I won't allow it."

Becca nods, looks a whole lot like she wants to start chewing on her newly manicured nails, and then glances out of the window again. I can't help but laugh. Now I guess I know exactly how she feels when she tells me to stop freaking out and I don't abide by her advice.

THE NEXT HALF HOUR ZOOMS BY IN RECORD SPEED. I'M talking, thirty minutes in less than five seconds. I don't know how it happens exactly, I have this theory involving time traveling cyborgs messing with the space-time continuum, but there's no time to think about that. Because one second I'm sitting at the vanity in the guest bedroom of Jace's inherited house, and the next second I hear the band playing and my mother rushes through the door, her eyes looking primed for crying, and says, "It's time!"

"What? No way!" I look for my cell phone but the thing is buried in my purse which is buried under suitcases and clothing and Aunt Truly's hair and makeup supplies. Frantically, I look around for Becca but no, of course she isn't here. She told me she was joining everyone on the back porch so they could get the ceremony started. It felt like she had said that just seconds ago, but I guess it was closer to fifteen minutes ago.

I don't have time to feel panic or anything as Mom rushes up and gives me a squeeze of a hug, carefully avoiding my hair and makeup. "Okay," I say, unable to hide my big goofy grin. "I guess it's time to do this thing."

We head into the hallway and walk toward the side door. Earlier they showed me how it was all set up: A white carpeted walkway leads from that door to the backyard, and then into the aisle where I'd meet Jace at the gazebo alter. Becca and Bentley will already be waiting next to Jace. And I guess, well, Jace's best friend Park won't be able to attend. I shrug off the disappointment I feel in being unable to surprise Jace. I'll have a lifetime of surprises to do. Right now it's time to get married.

Mom stops just at the end of the hall before the side door. She looks around. "Who's walking you down the aisle? What's Jace's dad's name again?"

"Huh?" I ask, feeling the warmth of dread and nerves creep up my spine.

Mom lifts a worried eyebrow. "Well, who's walking you? I figured you asked his dad too, since you don't exactly have a dad…Of course we could ask Grandpa, but he's sitting up at the front so he'd have to get his walker and come back down here…"

With a total disregard for my makeup, I slam my palm to my forehead. The aisle. The father giving away the groom. In all of our careful planning and late nights spent filling out that wedding notebook, how had we forgotten that I'd need someone to walk me down the freaking aisle?

Mom takes a bouquet of purple and turquoise roses from the shelf next to the door and hands them to me. My wedding bouquet. I didn't forget I'd need this. I shake my head slowly and fight like hell to keep the tears out of my eyes. "I completely forgot to ask anyone to walk me down the aisle," I say, my voice cracking at the last few words. "How could I have been so stupid?"

Mom looks genuinely surprised, and I think a little flash of fear even flickers across her face. I expect her to volunteer to do it, to walk me as if she were my father since she raised me alone. But she doesn't. She grabs my hand in hers and looks me straight in the eyes.

"Bayleigh, you are a strong girl. You can do absolutely anything you want to. I don't see why you can't walk down the aisle yourself. You chose Jace—you can choose to meet him your way."

"Yeah, I guess," I mumble, kicking at the hardwood flooring with my shoes.

"Excuse me," a male voice says from the end of the hallway. Mom and I jump at the same time, both turning to see who just walked in on our conversation. He's tall, at least as tall as Jace. And handsome in that classic way. He's wearing a black tux with a turquoise tie. I don't know why it takes me so long to figure out who this guy is—but I blame my air headedness on a massive amount of wedding anxiety. The man steps forward and holds out his hand. "Did I overhear a bride saying she has no one to walk her down the aisle?" He flashes me a million dollar smile. "Maybe I can help?"

I smile. "Park," I say warmly, reaching out for his hand. But instead of shaking my hand, he leans in for a hug. He smells like he's fresh out of the shower and not like he had been driving for the last twenty four hours.

"Did you just get here?" I ask.

He nods. "There was a massive wreck on Interstate forty-five. I lost an hour trying to get around that. Also...my truck is parked in the driveway even though we're all supposed to park in the lot next door. I knew how late I was and I didn't want to miss it."

"No worries," I say, grabbing onto his arm again. "I can't believe you're here. This is going to be so awesome for Jace." A renewed sense of excitement fills the air as Jace's best friend smiles back at me.

I glance at Mom and am happy to see that she looks just as excited as I do. She introduces herself to Park and then pulls him in for a hug, too. I guess this is an emotional time for all of us.

Pre-wedding music continues to play and as I glance at the clock on the wall, I am keenly aware that the guests outside are expecting me to walk out there any moment.

I turn toward Jace's best friend, biting on my bottom lip. It tastes like lipstick. "I would love for you to walk me down the aisle, if you don't mind."

He holds out his elbow and I take it. "It would be an absolute honor."

Mom opens the door and we step out onto the white carpet. I'm feeling wonderful until we turn around the house and I see a sea of family and friends all rise in their chairs and turn toward me. Now, I'm nervous. Excited. Crazy scared. Happy.

Now, I'm getting married.

Everyone looks at me as we walk. I only look at Jace. The expression on his face can be described as adoration when he first saw me, to shock, surprise and happiness when he noticed who was walking next to me. I glance up and sideways at Park and see him wink at Jace. Jace's tongue runs across his lips quickly and the dimples in his cheeks tell me that he's trying hard not to smile like a dork.

We take two steps up the gazebo, and when we reach Jace, Park takes my hand and puts it in Jace's hand. "She's all yours, bro."

The minister begins speaking but I'm too enchanted with staring into Jace's eyes to hear anything he says. Jace squeezes my hands at a couple of parts in the minister's speech. Realizing that it's my own wedding, and that I can always stare into Jace's blue eyes when it's over, I pull my gaze off of him and glance at the minister as he reads a passage about love from the Bible.

When he's finished, he tells the audience that we've written our own vows. Jace goes first. I draw in a deep breath. He always remembered them better than I did when we were practicing. Now, he says the words we crafted together as if they were written on his heart:

"Bayleigh, on this day, I give you my heart. I promise to walk with you hand in hand, wherever life takes us. I promise to love and live and learn with you. On this day, I promise that I will forever be yours."

A single tear rolls down my cheek. The minister tells me to go next. I swallow the lump in my throat, take a deep breath and promise myself to Jace.

"Jace, on this day, I give you my heart. I promise to walk with you hand in hand, wherever life takes us. I promise to love and live and learn with you. On this day, I promise that I will forever be yours."

The minister speaks louder this time. "With the power vested in me, I pronounce you man and wife. Jace, son, you may now kiss your bride."

Jace wraps an arm around my waist and dips me low, kissing me as if it's the last chance he'll ever get. The audience explodes into applause but I only hear the beating of my own heart as I kiss the man who is now my husband.

CHAPTER 22

Jace and I sneak out of the reception around nine o'clock. Everyone's having such a great time dancing under the clear lights in the trees and enjoying the live band playing. I don't think anyone noticed that we were gone, and they probably won't for quite some time. I sent Mom and Becca a text so they wouldn't worry. Jace tells me to grab the bag I had packed and we sneak off, tiptoeing through the massive house and slipping out the front door unseen.

I am drunk on love and my heart overflows with happiness. I am Mrs. Jace Adams. I feel like there's not a damn thing on this earth that I couldn't do.

I lift up my dress, holding on to the tail as we sprint across the yard and into my grandparent's yard where Jace's truck is parked. He's reversed in the driveway so we can make a quick getaway.

I'm breathing hard when we reach the truck. Jace pulls open my door and kisses me before letting me climb inside. "You ready for our honeymoon?" he asks, his eyes full of wonder and mischief.

"I'd be even more ready if I knew where we were going!" I say, laughing.

"Well that's up to you, Mrs. Adams." Jace gives me a sly smile before starting up the truck. I'm not sure what he means by that. Up to me? This whole honeymoon was planned by him!

We hold hands as we drive. But the drive doesn't take nearly as long as I had expected it to. Salt Gap is out in the middle of nowhere...hours away from the big cities. So when Jace slows down, puts on his blinker for some random back road, I lift an eyebrow.

"Where are we going?" I ask.

"Horseshoe Bend Airport," he says. But I don't need an answer now because we're driving past a sign that says the same thing. That's when I see a few massive airplane hangars, and a small control tower.

"I've never even heard of this airport," I say, wondering where he's planned for us to fly to. We pull into a parking spot next to a hangar. I'm still wearing my wedding dress and everything, but I don't want to take it off. I want to remember this night forever.

A man meets us outside of a hangar, greeting Jace by name.. This is no commercial airline. My mouth falls open as I take in the sight of the private jet waiting in front of us. The majestic, massive aircraft is a pearly white with blue details painted on the tail. Our luggage is loaded into the jet and then we're allowed to board.

Stairs fold out from the side of the plane and Jace motions for me to go first. We step into a luxurious interior of vanilla colored leather chairs and wood grain detailing. I run my fingers along the back of a chair. There are only six chairs. We will be the only guests flying tonight. A private jet. A private trip. This is way too good to be true.

We meet Christopher, who is our pilot. Well, I meet

him. Jace has known him for years, apparently. He flew in from Los Angeles just this morning. After a little small talk, I can't help but ask the question that's been in my mind ever since we left the wedding.

"So where are we flying tonight?"

Christopher gives me a sly smile, but it's Jace that speaks up. "This is our jet for the next three weeks," he says. "And it's ready to take us wherever you'd like to go."

THE SUMMER UNPLUGGED SERIES

Part 1 - Summer Unplugged

Part 2 - Autumn Unlocked

Part 3 - Winter Untold

Part 4 - Spring Unleashed

Part 5 - The Beginning of Forever

Part 6 - Autumn Adventure

Part 7 - Winter Wonderful

Part 8 - The Girl with my Heart

Part 9 - Autumn Awakening

Part 10 - Winter Whirlwind

Part 11 - Unplugged Summer

Don't miss all of the spin-off series:

The Summer Series

The Believe in Love Series

The Team Loco Series

The Love on the Track Series

The Love at the Gym Series

The Summer Unplugged Epilogues

ABOUT THE AUTHOR

Amy Sparling is the *USA Today* bestselling author of books for teens and the teens at heart. She lives on the coast of Texas with her family, her spoiled rotten pets, and a huge pile of books. She graduated with a degree in English and has worked at a bookstore, coffee shop, and a fashion boutique. Her fashion skills aren't the best, but luckily she turned her love of coffee and books into a writing career that means she can work in her pajamas. Her favorite things are coffee, book boyfriends, and Netflix binges.

She started writing her own books in 2010 and now publishes several books a year. She also writes young adult and middle grade novels under the name Cheyanne Young.

Connect with her on at AmySparling.com